The Priest

THE PRIEST

A Novel by
Bill Schubart

Magic Hill Press

The Priest

A novel by Bill Schubart

The Priest © 2018 Bill Schubart

Also by Bill Schubart:

The Lamoille Stories – ISBN: 978-0-9897121-0-1

Fat People – ISBN: 978-0-615-39751-1

Panhead – ISBN: 978-0-9834852-6-1

I Am Baybie – ISBN: 978-0-9834852-9-2

Photographic Memory – ISBN: 978-0-9834852-8-5

The Lamoille Stories II – ISBN: 978-0-9897121-3-2

Lila & Theron – ISBN: 978-1-6826-1356-6

Published by Magic Hill Press LLC, 144 Magic Hill Road, Hinesburg, VT 05461
    magichillpress.com
Distributed by Ingram
MSRP $15.00. paperback / $9.99 EB
(168 pages)

Front cover and title page art: Sergio de Castro, *vitrail de Jonas* (detail).
    From a photograph by Dominique Souse
Design: Laughing Bear Associates
Literary editor: Madeleine Stone
Copy editor: Ruth Sylvester

ISBN#s:
    P.B. 978-0-9897121-8-7
    E.B. 978-0-9897121-9-4
Library of Congress Control #: 2018913034

In gratitude for insightful criticism: Steve Blodgett, Larry Connolly,
Father David Cray, Darcie Abbene, Andre LaChance, Marcela Lesan,
Will Patten, Kate Schubart, and Madeleine Stone.

This work was written while listening to Henryk Górecki's Symphony#3,
Opus 36, *Symphony of Sorrowful Songs*.

This is a work of fiction but like most works of fiction, it is based on
some real events and real people.

"Father, it's time for seven o'clock Mass."

An insistent knocking on the rectory door wakes me from a troubled sleep. My head is buzzing with a dull pressure and feels like it's stuffed with mattress wadding. I hear distant static and my rumpled bed smells. I'm surprised to see I'm naked, as I've always worn pajamas. I pull on a bathrobe and make my way to the door.

"Father, are you going to say Mass this morning?" asks my new altar boy, Billy Graves.

"I'm a bit under the weather, Billy. Would you make my apologies to anyone in the church, and I'll resume daily Mass tomorrow if I feel better."

"Okay, Father. I hope you feel better," Billy answers, surprised I've not opened the door beyond a crack.

I walk into the bathroom and relieve myself. I remember going into the kitchen and making a plate of cheese, cold cuts, and crackers that neither of us touched, as she refilled our glasses. I try to remember her leaving but can't.

My bed exudes an unfamiliar musky odor. Did we have sex? We can't have. I'm a Catholic priest sworn to celibacy. But through the fog of my first hangover, I see Ellen on top of me with her back arched and her head tossed way back. Her breasts graze my chest. It's an image I'll recall many times when I make love alone. She's making a low noise that suggests pain, but I've never had sex before and have no understanding of my role in either her pleasure or her pain.

I know myself well enough to doubt that I initiated this. Still, the familiar afterglow of masturbation suggests I've had sex with a woman for the first time. I'm confused and afraid. I've just been intimate with a woman I met in the confessional and am no longer celibate.

I strip the bed, ball up the linen, and stuff it into the washing machine in the next room. Realizing I've no idea how the machine works, I step into the cramped shower stall nearby and turn on the water. The first splash of cold water feels good and gradually warms to a comfortable temperature. I imagine myself trying to wash away my sins like the early penitents in *The Lives of the Saints*.

Dry now and in my cassock and Roman collar, I pull the bedspread over my exposed mattress, fold my unused pajamas as Ma taught me, and lay them on the bed.

In the kitchen, I drop two pieces of cottony bread into the toaster, depress the handle, and boil water for instant coffee. I've only been a priest for eighteen months and have already broken my promise to God and my Church.

I see the note on the kitchen table, the folded edge of which is tucked under the sugar bowl. I sit down and open the note. I look at the bottom first where it says only "Ellen."

Father Pierre,

I hope you enjoyed last night. In coming to talk with you, it was never my intent that we would sleep together. Please believe this… I'm not a wanton woman and, apart from my husband and the man I'm going to, you're the only other man I've ever made love with.

I appreciated your hearing me out and your compassion. I'll do the penance you gave me every day. Your absolution is the

greatest gift you could have ever given me. I'll stay in our faith,
even as I know there are no priests who would ever forgive me for
what I'm doing or for what we did last night.

You must believe me when I say I never planned or imagined
this. I was so struck by the sadness and loneliness of the life you
described, my instincts to comfort you overwhelmed my better
judgment and then turned sexual, which came as a surprise to
both of us, I suspect.

The gratitude and pleasure with which you received my
caresses felt like permission for us to make love, which I've no
wish to repeat but will never forget.

You're a kind and wonderful man. I don't expect our paths to
ever cross again but am grateful they did.

I'm leaving tonight for Newton, Mass, where I'll live out the
rest of my life I suspect.

Thank you again for your compassion, forgiveness, and
great kindness. I hope your life ahead is more joyful.

Ellen

With a dull ache in the back of my head and an acrid taste in
my mouth, I pour a coffee and re-read the letter. She must have left
early this morning before I awoke. Why does she use the phrase "made
love?" I've never loved a woman that way, and I don't know what "made
love" means.

Fragments of memory tell me I was complicit and can't blame the
woman named Ellen. I can't remember the course our discussion took
beforehand or how I rationalized her absolution. What penance did I
invoke? Was it a one-time penance or a daily one?

My Early Calling

I decided to become a priest when I was twelve. What little I'd heard on the playground about sex and how babies were conceived terrified me. When I made up my child's mind to become a priest, I'd been abusing myself for a year and confessing my sins weekly, so I would not go to hell if I were to die suddenly.

My first sensations of arousal began when I graduated from the infantile world of the bathtub to the privacy and maturity of a shower, sometime in fifth grade. The surprising sensations came from soaping myself all over and scrubbing "my dirty parts," as I had been taught by my mother. The unfocused sensation was pleasant, and I often luxuriated in the shower until called out by a parent. Since I slept in the same room as my older brother Rosaire, the shower was my only private place as a child.

In Saturday catechism, Sister Thérèse made clear to us that dying with the sin of self-abuse on our soul meant an eternity of hell-fire. To ensure our understanding of hell as the penalty for self-abuse, she asked, "How many of you ever burned your hand on a kitchen stove or wood stove?" We all raised our hands. "Now imagine that pain over all your body for eternity and you will understand what hell will be like if you die with a mortal sin on your soul." We were all terrified.

When I was eight, the house three doors down from us caught fire in the middle of the night and burned to the ground. It was one of the first houses in our neighborhood to be electrified, having been heated by a wood-fired furnace in the basement for seventy years. We assumed the novelty of electrical wiring started the fire, although it was never proven. The firemen worked through the night to keep the neighboring houses from catching fire, as the house itself was too far gone to be saved. We heard that Selma Travers died in the fire. Although we only saw her at church, we knew her as a kindly lady who gave alms to the poor and spent summers knitting on her expansive front porch and offering passers-by a glass of her home-made lemonade. Her nephew Buford was in the fire brigade and ran into the burning house to try to save her but died when the second floor collapsed. A boy at school described the charred remains he saw as he walked by the house the following day. His description brought further to life the horrors that we would experience if we were to die with a mortal sin on our soul.

Like Rosaire, I became an altar boy in third grade. I soon mastered the choreography of serving Mass — when to kneel and stand and where to be in relation to the priest I was serving. I memorized the Latin liturgy and the Ordinary of a Low Mass from the Introit to the Sanctus, Consecration, Communion, and Final Blessing.

Our days began at six, Sunday dinners at noon, supper at five, and lights out by nine. On Sunday, I usually served the eight o'clock Mass. It was better attended than the ten o'clock. Before going into the vestry and putting on my altar boy's cassock and surplice, I'd slip through the curtains into the left side of the confessional, its vacancy evidenced by the drawn-back curtain. I'd pull the curtain closed and kneel on the un-upholstered kneeler. On this day, the confessional was redolent with Laurette Piette's perfume; I'd just seen her emerge from the confessional.

The dry sound of the slide moving back and the silhouette of Father Delaire seated behind the wooden grillwork signaled the beginning of my confession, which I'd always plan out the night before.

"Bless me Father for it's been one week since my last confession. I accuse myself of lying to my mother once about doing my homework, being mean to a friend at school, and abusing myself two times. For these and all the sins I cannot now remember, I ask God's pardon and your absolution, Father."

"Do you have dirty thoughts when you abuse yourself, my son?"

"I do, father."

"You must pray to the Holy Virgin for purity of thought and mind and, for your penance, say an Act of Contrition and ten Hail Marys."

"Thank you, Father, I will."

The slide would close, I'd stand up, open the curtain, and go into the sacristy. Father Delaire would follow me and begin immediately to don the vestments for Epiphany while I pulled the white starched surplice over my head and smoothed it out over my cassock. The other altar boy assigned to eight o'clock Mass was Warren, who was waiting for us.

Warren and I would walk ahead of Father Delaire into the sanctuary without looking at the crowded pews, genuflect before the Tabernacle, and kneel to begin the Ordinary of the Mass.

Sometimes when I was alone at home I'd pretend to be a priest, using the side table as an altar and moving the coffee table in front to the side for the Lavabo and the mixing of the water and wine. I knew the celebrant's movements by heart and acted out the main parts of the Mass. After the Consecration, I'd offer Communion, and then a final benediction with the words, "Ite, Missa est... Go, the Mass is ended."

Once, Rosaire burst in on me and made fun of me. He could see what I was up to. He promised not to say anything but, of course, he did and I heard about it at school, where the older kids started calling me "Father Pierre."

My younger sister Lucienne and I took our schoolwork seriously. Rosaire did just enough to get by and graduate. As early as I can remember, he wanted to join the army and drive heavy equipment. Pa fought in World War I but never spoke of his service in the war or his time in the trenches at Belleau Wood with mustard gas canisters falling around him. Sometimes, he'd wake up screaming in the night and Ma would have to calm him down. Although he talked little about his military experience. he always urged Rosaire to enlist in the air force, warning him to steer clear of both the army and the navy and take up flying. At least in the air, he said, you'll have a chance. But Rosaire had his own ideas and, by the time he entered high school, he and Pa no longer spoke about military service.

Rosaire was nice to me, but I always thought he saw me as weak and unwilling to take life on. At about the same time, I began noticing girls at school and listening to older boys on the playground talk about them in a way I didn't understand. I knew girls were different from boys, as I had seen my mother change my baby sister's diapers.

My parents only spoke of sex in the abstract, alluding to its purpose of "making babies." It happened only between married couples. I could make no connection between the security, warmth, and pleasure I felt under a deluge of warm water behind the privacy of a shower curtain and the mothers in town laboring through the grocery store straining against the counterweight of a late pregnancy.

Given the lectures I'd heard at home, school, and catechism on modesty and hygiene, the idea that nature's design enabled sex seemed unimaginable. The older playground boys, though, seemed to be experts on the subject and spoke graphically of their considerable experience with girls. I was naïve enough to believe what I heard, making the whole prospect of sex more terrifying and unnatural.

I understood that priests could never marry or have children and so chose that vocation when I was twelve — hardly the spiritual epiphany we read about in *The Lives of the Saints* — but more a flight from the childhood fears made vivid by Sister Thérèse in catechism and the older boys on the playground.

The solemnity and consistency of the Catholic Mass — its processions, vestments, evocative statues, commandments, sacraments, and feast days, in which I was a regular acolyte — offered a reassuring alternative to the demands I would suffer as an adult expected to "go forth and multiply."

Cabot, Vermont 1934

Our house, like many on Congress Street in Cabot, needs paint. Water stains icicle the white paint below the eaves, and whitecaps of flaking paint surround the window frames. The new school bus stops on the corner of Thorndike Street, so my schoolmates can't see our peeling paint, sagging porch, and broken garage door, not that many of their houses don't look the same. Each day I walk past the charred remains of Selma's house and recall Sister Thérèse's vivid description of hell.

My father works at the Chambers Granite sheds in nearby Barre. He's a stone cutter and spends his days hovering over a pneumatic drill, then hammering cut lines with a tracer and pounding feathers and wedges into the holes he's drilled to split the large blocks of granite later carved and polished into memorials or building blocks. The pneumatic drill has destroyed most of his hearing, although he rigorously denies his deafness, insisting instead that we all mumble. His own voice is raspy from the mustard gas he inhaled in the war.

Ma's a maid at the Phillips estate. At home, she wears a threadbare cotton dress mottled with permanent kitchen stains — a pointillist canvas of countless Sunday dinners. When she leaves for work at 7:30 in her lacy apron-fronted white skirt with red trim, her frilly blouse and maid's cap after making us all an early breakfast, she reminds me of a carnation. On leaving, she curtsies to us in mock deference to the world she's about to enter. Hiding her maid's uniform under the woolen coat she's had since 1923, when she quit eleventh grade to give birth to

Rosaire, she disappears around the corner of our house to catch the jitney to Mr. Phillips's estate in Montpelier. Pa sleeps in and leaves an hour later. Weekends, he augments his income pumping gas at a local Esso station, cleaning windshields and checking oil for patrons. He too suffers the indignity of a silly white uniform and logo'd cap, both permanently stained with grease and oil.

We see Pa only at church and at night before he falls asleep in his chair after dinner. My earliest memories are of him telling us made-up stories in his raspy voice, often accompanied by a musical ditty, but lately he's too tired and goes from the dinner table silence to his chair where he falls asleep with a cigarette that one of us will pluck from his lips before the ash falls or burns his lips and wakes him.

Rosaire sleeps in the bed next to the witch window, and I sleep in an army cot against the wall. I used to have my own room until Lucienne was born and then I moved in with Rosaire who already fancies himself a man with little time or patience for a younger brother, while little Lucienne shares our mother's sweetness. She and I always get along well.

At eleven, I enter sixth grade. I like school, but not all the rough-housing and teasing at recess. We all go outside at the recess bell, except when it's raining hard. Since the older boys compete by ganging up on younger kids, I'd rather stay in study hall and read. Outside, I try to keep to myself. In winter, the big kids play *king of the mountain* and fight each other to see who can stay on top of the large snowbank the plow pushes to one corner of the playground. Their favorite way of picking on us younger kids is to shout, "dirty face, dirty face," and then rub snow in our face and neck. It melts into our clothes and leaves us wet for the rest of the school day. Teachers take turns monitoring our recess play, but mostly stand inside the storm door and smoke.

I see Lucienne in the lunchroom and we often sit together and talk about what we're learning or who's absent from school and why. She worries about Pa and I see tears in her eyes when she talks about him. It's in the cafeteria that I first hear her talk about Pa dying, as if she knows he's going to die, whereas I always just assumed he was sick and would get better. It never occurred to me Pa could die.

The Phillips Estate

Every year, Mr. and Mrs. Phillips invite the help and their families to the estate for Boxing Day. None of us had ever heard of Boxing Day before Ma started working there. To us, it seems like a second Christmas, and the food and the gifts exceed what we expect in our own Christmas celebration the day before. Even Rosaire looks forward to it. It's the one day Ma doesn't have to wear her silly little maid's outfit. She puts on her Sunday dress and does up her hair. Pa wears his Sunday suit and Ma trims his hair and beard. Pa thinks it's humiliating to accept the charity of "rich people" but always accedes to Ma's insistence that we appear as a family for her job security, worrying that the Phillips might be offended if we don't accept their seasonal largesse.

The Phillips estate is on the outskirts of Montpelier, an imposing Georgian house that looks to us like a castle. Rosaire mows our small lawn with a rusty push mower every week in twenty minutes and marvels at how long it must take to mow the vast lawn that aprons the main house. The large stable behind the house has been converted to garages for the various cars and antique coaches the Phillips family have used over the years. A 1928 Dodge Victory Six touring car glistens on the crushed stone drive in front of the garage, alongside a dark green 1934 Massey-Harris orchard tractor with steel wheels. Open garage doors allow for a glimpse at the gleaming black postilion landau coach parked inside, two open buckboards, and an old threshing machine.

As we walk up the fieldstone steps to the main entrance, Ma waves to other Phillips domestics arriving for the party. She seems more light-hearted than I'm used to seeing and hushes Pa's grumblings.

"It's just for two hours. You can eat all you want," she encourages him.

"They'se teetotalers, won't be no drink I 'spect."

"Yes, but there'll be plenty to eat, and you can have a beer when we get home. Try and enjoy yourself for the kids."

As Lucienne and I approach the front door, followed by Ma, Pa, and Rosaire, it's opened by Mr. Phillips himself before Ma can lift the shining brass knocker in the middle. After a warm holiday greeting and handshake, he wishes us all a Merry Christmas, shakes hands with Ma and Pa, and ushers us into the marble entryway, the smell of roast poultry and baked goods wafting through the door.

Rosaire excuses himself to go out back and ogle the various vehicles arrayed in their garages. We're invited to hang our coats in the front hall closet and go into the main living space that arises cathedral-like two stories to the ceiling. There are no servants in sight. A linen-covered banquet table displays platters of duck and ham. A crystal punchbowl presides over the middle of the table, flanked by two lit silver candelabra.

We're always be among the early arrivals, and Ma immediately begins chatting with another maid, Millie, and the Phillips' cook, Sandra. Unable to hear most conversation, Pa joins Rosaire out back while Lucienne and I stare at the vast space above us. A crystal chandelier the size of a granite saw hangs from two stories above. The room we're in is flanked on three sides by surrounding mezzanines on the second and third levels. The bedroom doors on the second mezzanine are far apart, indicating large bedrooms for family and guests. On the third-floor mezzanine, the doors are closer together, indicating servants' quarters. The second floor over the main entrance is a vast open library with floor-to-ceiling bookshelves and a black walnut track-ladder with polished brass treads. To Lucienne and me, the house never loses its capacity to inspire awe and to evoke another world which we can only imagine inhabiting.

We heap our plates with food and find a place to perch and eat. Rosaire always goes back for seconds. Pa eats one full plate and returns his plate to the sideboard, too proud to have seconds. With a filigreed silver cake server, Lucienne and I each fork a slice of *bûche de Noël* onto our small china plates. This is Ma's favorite and we watch her savoring each forkful.

Each night after dinner, Lucienne and I take turns washing up and putting food away while Pa retires to his chair and Ma sits on the couch reading hand-me-down magazines from her work. At the Phillips estate I ask her, "If all the servants are guests, who'll wash all these dishes and clean up?" I know how long it takes to wash the few dishes and utensils that we use each night at supper. The Phillips estate employs over sixteen domestics in different capacities, and I imagine a kitchen overflowing with dirty china and silver.

"Millie and her crew will clean up tomorrow. None of us are working today. That's the tradition," Ma answers.

As a maid, Ma works mostly around the house, cleaning, dusting, ironing, and folding household linens with a large mangle iron. The linens are kept in a mothproof vault she once showed me, next to a matching vault that secures silver, crystal, and china. The only other vault I'd seen that size was the one in Mr. Chambers' office at the Granite Company.

After we all eat our fill, Mrs. Phillips leads us all in singing a few Christmas carols. Sitting at the ebony Bechstein grand piano in the living room, she accompanies us with chords, which seem to cheer all except Pa who's gone back outside. A ten-foot Christmas tree shelters dozens of brightly wrapped but unmarked gift baskets. Each family is invited to take one. We knew what's inside from earlier years.

At four, as the sky darkens, Mr. and Mrs. Phillips go to the front door to receive the thanks and best wishes of their departing guests. Unlike Pa and Rosaire, Ma, Lucienne, and I believe the Phillips' good wishes to be sincere and well-meaning. We welcome their gratitude, as we appreciate their employment and their kindness.

On the way home, Lucienne falls asleep on my shoulder. Pa is silent and Rosaire chatters on about the tractor and the elegant town car. Ma hums a carol quietly to herself.

At home, Rosaire and I bring in several armloads of firewood, and Pa stirs and stokes the embers in the woodstove. As the house warms up, Ma puts away the small canned ham, shortbread biscuits, and slides the ten-dollar bill into the coffee can in which she keeps spare change for groceries.

Pa settles into his chair and nurses a Carling Black Label beer, a Chesterfield dangling from his lips. Rosaire retreats to his room with a J.C. Whitney car parts catalog he's pilfered in one of the garages. Lucienne and I sit at the table, regaling one another with descriptions of the unimaginable wealth we've just seen.

Catechism

Although I like serving Mass, I have mixed feelings about catechism. The nuns speak mostly French but for the few Irish and Italian kids, they also speak in their labored Québecois English. Sister Agnès is young and I sometimes daydream about what's obscured by her wimple and habit. Sister Thérèse is in her sixties and stricter but always ends her moral admonitions with a benign and finely wrinkled smile that puts us at ease.

Our text is the Baltimore Catechism. Unlike at school where we flit from subject to subject and are asked to draw conclusions from what we've learned, the absolutes in catechism are comforting. Sin, we learn, is a binary concept of good and evil.

My mind often drifts, and I see Sister Agnès as my guardian angel as if she was watching over me in my bed at home, her beatific face framed tightly at the temples by a starched white wimple, and her blue linen tunic suggesting the gentle rise of girlish breasts. I imagine light brown hair falling loose over her translucent skin gathered in a smile that notices but forgives, if not welcomes, my regard. I look away embarrassed at being caught staring. She smiles, and I'm left haunted by the conflict between her lectures on purity of thought and the young girl I imagine beneath her habit. A question from Sister Thérèse jolts me back into the church basement and catechism class.

Her lengthy disquisitions on love, marriage, and chastity only feed my fear of becoming an adult. She often uses the word "cupidity", which I look up in my dictionary at home and find to mean "physical desire."

While Sister Agnès seems too young to instruct us on sex and marriage, Sister Thérèse seems too old to do so, but nonetheless chatters on about purity of thought and habit, self-abuse, and the evils of sex before marriage while the boys in my class smirk at one another.

Mostly, the commandments make sense to me... . "Thou shalt not kill, commit adultery, steal, bear false witness," but I find the ninth and tenth commandments confusing. When I ask about them, Sister Thérèse explains that to *covet* doesn't mean *to take* but *to want* or *be jealous of*, further confusing me as I've always experienced desire as being beyond the bounds of free will and only becoming a sin when I act on it as I do when I abuse myself. To this day, I still struggle with the distinction between desire and deed when my parishioners confess their sins.

I once asked Sister Thérèse, "Since divorce and remarriage can never be absolved in confession, as it's a "sin of persistence," wouldn't killing one's former spouse and seeking absolution for murder be a surer path to redemption in a broken marriage?" I expected an angry reaction but got only her benign smile. She affirmed my logic, but denied my conclusion, saying, "No priest would ever absolve such a calculated sin." Her logic eluded me.

Even though the few priests and nuns I know leave no room for ambiguity in their moral teaching, catechism seems fraught with ethical ambiguities I pray will clarify themselves when I finally become a priest.

We're Alone Now

Pa's finding it harder to hear. He gets angry at whoever's talking to him because he can't make out what they're saying and grumbles that, "No'ne speaks clear anymore." He begins talking more loudly to compensate and we hear anger where there's only fear. Ma explains that Pa's proud and finds it hard to admit to his increasing deafness.

Eventually, his boss notes the severity of his hearing and, for safety reasons, reassigns him from hammer-drilling, tracing, and splitting in the open quarry to the sawing and polishing shed. Only younger men are trained to operate the massive granite saw, so at forty-two, Pa's reassigned to an air-driven grinder/buffer, fine-finishing rough-cut granite.

Not long after beginning work in the sheds, his breathing becomes more labored. He denies this, too, and rarely talks anymore during supper, as even conversation seems to wind him, as he gulps air in between his phrases. After supper, we hear him wheezing and sometimes gasping for air on the couch. Ma wants him to see the company doctor, but he insists that nothing's wrong and that it's just a result of his wartime exposure to mustard gas. Ma explains to us that Pa knows if he complains to the company doctor about breathing problems, he'll be laid off like his coworkers. Granite workers working in the sawing and polishing sheds, she explains, get silicosis and, as soon as they exhibit breathing problems, the company wants them off the payroll before the disease becomes a liability. Silicosis is understood legally as work-related, so the company could be held liable for unsafe working conditions and be required to provide monetary benefits to those afflicted. Even back then it was generally understood that smoking was unhealthy, and Pa still smokes. Ma begs him to give up his Chesterfields, but he'd waves her off, dismissing her fears.

"One a' my few pleasures…" he'd mutters.

"What will become of us if you get sick and can't work?" she'd asks.

"I can work, always have ha'n't I? Never let you and the kids down. Paycheck keeps coming. You din't have to work, you chose to. I've always been the breadwinner and always will be."

The conversation always ends there. I see the fear in Ma's eyes as she turns away from her husband of twenty years. She knows how this will play out. She's seen it in too many of her friends' husbands who work in the sheds. Smoking only hastens the end.

After he's laid off, it takes Pa fourteen months to die. Most of that time he lies at home in their bed. Ma begins sleeping in the next room with Lucienne, but she can still hear Pa's efforts to breathe through the plaster wall.

One night, we visit Pa after Ma's removed his untouched supper tray. Pa was always compact and heavily muscled from his work in the quarry. But as we stare aghast at the wraith barely disturbing a cotton sheet and patchwork quilt, we understand how thoroughly the fine dust in the shed has diminished the robust man we once knew. Ma tells us not to show our shock at the skeletal face we see lying sideways on a pillow. His cheek and chin bones protrude beneath the parchment-like skin. His coughs have lost their violence, subsiding to gurgles and an occasional gulp for air. Lucienne and I don't know this dying man. Rosaire always finds reasons not to go into Pa's room.

As children we aren't spared the ravages of death. When Ma's mother Laurette lay dying of a series of strokes, we visited her every week. The trip was an hour each way. The strokes had distorted her face, her hands curled like monkey paws, and only Ma could make sense of her utterances. The stroke had not affected her mind but had effectively isolated her, compounding her sense of loneliness. Ma understood this and made every effort to communicate. We stood by while Ma tried to carry on a conversation with her, mostly delivering news of our comings and goings, successes in school, or lack thereof, and Pa's work in the quarries. At Ma-mère's funeral, we solemnly walked by her open casket, each taking a few minutes to kneel at the prie-dieu in front and pay our last respects. Ma was the last to go and reached in to hold her mother's hands in prayer as she said goodbye. When she arose, she leaned in and kissed Ma-mère on the forehead.

Dr. Lepine comes every two weeks and brings laudanum for Pa. We stay out of the room while he and Ma whisper to one another about Pa's decline. When our turn comes to visit, we just stand and watch fearfully as Pa drowns slowly in the fluids filling his lungs. Dr. Lepine assures Ma that when the end is near, Pa won't suffer.

Two days later during his next visit, he goes into Pa's room alone and when he comes out to report to us on Pa's condition, he look at us all and says only, "Your father's gone."

We understand Pa is dead. Only later do I learn that Pa's death was a benevolent violation of the fifth commandment.

Hope Cemetery

Pa's funeral is like most Catholic funerals of the time, a wake or "viewing" and a solemn high funeral Mass the following day at which Rosaire and I assist as altar boys. Five colleagues from the quarries and Rosaire bear Pa's body to the hearse after Mass ends, and we all follow in a black-car cortege to Hope Cemetery.

When I was six, Pa has taken us on a tour of the carved granite statuary that graced the hillside cemetery. Hope Cemetery was the pride of the granite industry, and Pa knew many of the artisans who had designed and carved some of its finer works. As we ambled through the forested sculpture gallery, Pa pointed out his favorite carver, Louis Brusa, whose "Bored Angel" and "The Dying Man" drew visitors from all over the world. Brusa had died a generation earlier of silicosis.

The cortege winds around the cemetery until we stop near a freshly dug gravesite. Pa's coworkers had etched a modest upright granite memorial from stone donated by Chambers Granite.

Alphonse Carrier, né 1898, allé a son créateur 1943

We emerge from the car and walk behind Ma to the rectangular hole and the adjacent mound of gravel. My first sense on looking down into the grave is of unrelenting cold. Pa's bearers carry his casket over and hold it over the two ropes they use to lower it into the hole. As they lower Pa into the ground, feeding out the rope hand-over-hand, Ma cries softly. We try to mask our fears in reverence. Ma tosses a bouquet on top of the coffin, and friends and colleagues toss in hand-fuls of gravel. The pebbles make a hollow sound bouncing off the coffin. In retrospect, I'm surprised at the vacancy of my own sadness. I can't speak for Rosaire and Lucienne, but my strongest memory is of fear — fear of what's to become of us.

For the first time, I notice the Phillips' two-tone Rover parked near the end of the cortege. Their dark-suited chauffeur sits inside, the engine idling in the cold. I scan the crowd and see Mr. and Mrs. Phillips standing at the rear of the small gathering of their domestics alongside Pa's colleagues from the sheds who've come to pay their final respects.

Back at home, a few of Ma and Pa's friends stop by to offer con-dolences and ask if they can be of help and to assure themselves we'll be okay.

Rosaire excuses himself and leaves. Lucienne and I change out of our funeral dress and busy ourselves in the kitchen. Ma in her black dress and veil sits on the couch, staring straight ahead. I've never seen her look this way. I go over and sit down next to her, putting my hand in her lap. After a few seconds, she notices me, turns, and smiles through her tears.

"What will we do?" I ask.

"We'll get by," she replies, looking away.

I can't apply any scale to her response. Does it mean we'll survive the pain of Pa's death or of being poor? I'd heard the phrase "get by" all my life but realize for the first time I have no idea what it means.

Getting By

Father Delaire visits us to see how we're doing. He usually brings a loaf of bread, a cooked ham, or two cans of baked beans. Ma thanks him but assures him we're getting on okay.

Rosaire, who's been haunting the local army recruiting office in Barre, comes home one night and announces he's quit school and taken a full-time job at the Phillips Estate as an assistant groundskeeper. His job entails trimming the carefully-sculpted hedges, weeding the flower beds, and mowing their expansive lawns with their new Gravely mowing machine, not the heavy equipment he pined for, but larger than the push-mower he struggles with at home.

Not consulted, Ma greets this news with mixed feelings. Rosaire's taken it on himself to ask Mr. Phillips for the job, knowing full well his affection for her. A few days later, Mr. Phillips invites Ma to work extra hours should she need to, and Ma expresses her gratitude to him, wondering what Rosaire might have said to him.

With two years to go before graduation, my plans to become a priest are dashed when I learn that I'll need a college degree to be accepted into any seminary.

I ask to meet with Father Delaire who knows of my vocational aspiration and has been supportive. He contacts the bishop's office in Burlington and determines that St. John's Seminary in Massachusetts offers both a Bachelor of Theology and a post-graduate Master of Divinity degree, which would enable me to take Holy Orders.

Father Delaire further adds that the bishop is pleased to hear of my commitment and will gladly sponsor me as a candidate if my high school grades earn me acceptance to St. John's.

The news is encouraging, but I wonder how I can achieve my plan to become a priest and go to seminary, which will cost nothing, but will also pay nothing, either. It will be another eight years before I earn the modest stipend of a parish priest. I know Ma will have only herself and Lucienne to provide for when Rosaire and I leave home, but for now, we're still four mouths to feed. I ask the manager of the Esso station if I might take over Pa's job, which doesn't conflict with school, and he agrees.

We keep on through two difficult years. It's clear though that, even with Ma's, Rosaire's, and my modest income, Ma will have to sell the house. Lack of any maintenance has lowered its value to less than a thousand dollars above the outstanding mortgage and the market for houses in our neighborhood is soft. There's no way to know how long it might take to sell it, or whether it would produce any savings for Ma.

Ma's brother, Morris, dies in the late fall and her sister-in-law Jeanine, who teaches fourth grade in nearby Marshfield, offers to move in with Ma and share living expenses. Widowed, she can no longer afford to maintain her house on a teacher's salary. Ma discusses the matter with us and we all agree. It's a practical solution. Ma likes Jeanine and, when Morris's kidney failure forced him to quit carpentry work, Ma often made the trip alone to help Jeanine out.

After Morris's funeral, Jeanine moves in with us. She has her own room. Ma and Lucienne share their room and Rosaire and I continue to share. Jeanine is told that there's little point in listing her house in such a down market but that renting it might prove easy. Her rental and teaching income combine to make our household viable. We're all relieved at our good fortune and at Jeanine's good will.

The following year, with the blessing of the bishop's vocational director, I apply to St. John's Seminary in Brighton, Massachusetts and am accepted.

A Seminarian's Life

My years in seminary are some of the happiest in my life. Freed from the fraternal pressure and hedonistic bravado of boys pretending to be men and the sensual distractions of girls becoming women, I finally feel safe and concentrate on becoming a priest. I have privacy when I need it and social contact when I want it. I still masturbate and fear the persistence of this mortal sin to which I must confess weekly to my Father-confessor at St. John's. I'm afraid he'll judge me unsuitable to my chosen vocation.

Our cells are austere, furnished only with a wood-frame bed, a spindly desk, a bookcase, a ladder-back chair and a crucifix hanging over the headboard. When I feel the urge to masturbate, I remove the crucifix from its nail over my headboard and hide it in my desk drawer. As a child, I'd worried that the picture on Rosaire's bookcase of Ma and Pa taken shortly after they were married looking straight into the camera meant they could see what I was up to under my bedspread.

In my first year, I sign up for Fundamental Theology, Pastoral Duties, Principles of Moral Theology, History and Theology of Liturgy, and Methodology of Biblical Studies — a full course load for a novice. I soon learn how simplistic my catechism knowledge of Catholicism is.

I miss Lucienne, Ma, and even Rosaire, who at 22, is now in basic training at Fort Knox. I know from Ma and Lucienne's letters that their lives have settled into a spare but comfortable routine. Lucienne's already a junior, doing well in her studies, and like Aunt Jeanine, has decided to become a teacher of history and civics. Ma's been promoted at the Phillips Estate and now oversees the entire housekeeping staff. Mrs. Phillips asks her periodically how she's getting on at home and encourages her to ask for help should she ever need it, but Ma's pride would never have allowed her to admit to such a need. The security of knowing that help is offered, however, comforts her.

I make the annual six-hour bus trip home for Christmas and Easter until, in my third year, I'm pressed into service at a parish outside Boston to help during the Christmas season.

In my final year, I study Church Administration, Theology of the Laity for Pastoral Ministry, Canon Law, Homiletics, and The Literature of the Psalms. I'm also assigned a supervised parish internship. Even though there's a fraternal camaraderie among the novices, I make few close friends during my years in seminary. I'm known as a loner. People like me yet pay little attention to me. I'm not invited into the various cliques, sports play, and study groups that to my surprise abound there.

My only close confidant is Paolo Barza. Paolo was raised in a Portuguese fishing family in Gloucester but suspects he was adopted from another wing of the family. Pressed into service on his father's trawler from the age of ten, he never takes to the sea, often feeling seasick. He's teased by his older brother who loves fishing and shamed by his father for his queasiness in rough weather and while scaling and gutting the day's catch. Paolo and I spend many hours in the quiet evening hours after vespers discussing the relevance of church teaching to the lives we lead.

To this day, St. John's Seminary follows the monastic *Liturgy of the Hours: Matins, Lauds, Prime, Terce, Sext, None, Vespers,* and

Compline. My favorite, *Vespers*, comes during the last light of day. The only light in the chapel is from the sanctuary lamp by the altar and the evanescent rays of almost tangible sunlight that stream through the clerestory windows high above our pews. Vespers is the only one of the hours we sing as a full community in plainsong. I remember hearing from my uncle Arsène Cottard from Nova Scotia that my favorite, *Ave Maris Stella*, is also the anthem of Acadian fishermen. The waning light and unaccompanied voices of men intoning odes of praise that reverberate through the lofty emptiness above imbue in me a peace I doubt I'll know again.

In our whispered conversations, Paolo and I discover we've each chosen the priesthood in part as a refuge from the sexual confusion we both feel as young men. What seems so natural to our eager companions remains paradoxical to us. Although hardly immune to the temptations of the flesh, we dread the sexual innuendos of the few girls who approach us, knowing we're expected to react in some way we don't understand. At first, we discuss it uncomfortably until we understand it as one of our many common bonds. Mostly we talk over what we're learning in seminary and what it will be like when we became priests and have parishes and a flock of our own to care for.

Although my years in seminary instill in me a deep appreciation for silence and emptiness, my solitude is still haunted by doubts. Perhaps I read too much history.

My senior advisor, Father Arthur, is a scholar in Church history and an eager student of the martyrdom of the desert fathers, medieval flagellants, and the Spanish Inquisition. Often as we share an evening tea, he regales me with the excesses of the Church up through the Crusades, always careful to remind me that the horrors Mother Church perpetrated on the unfaithful were the inspiration of men, not

God. In his telling, it seems most ecclesiastical torture was visited on women. Obsessed with allegations of sexual transgressions visited on godly men by bedeviled women, certain priests and cardinals invented ever more salacious tortures to indulge their sadistic fantasies. Father Arthur never brings up, however, the centuries of child sexual abuse, nor the hierarchy's truculent defense and sheltering of perpetrators on the few early occasions when such abuses came to light.

My doubts persist, and I confess them as sins to my Father-confessor. For my penance, he orders me to walk the *Camino de Santiago* before taking my Holy Orders.

During my final break, I borrow money from Ma and book round-trip passage to Cherbourg on a freighter, sharing four bunks with a trio of Norwegian sailors returning home. I begin in Tours, spending my first week fulfilling a promise to my patron saint to pray a novena in the Basilica of St. Martin. Like many young men, I expressed no fear of military conflict, at least as we saw it in the movies — heroic and painless — but was afraid of communal living, lack of privacy, and being teased.

In catechism, we'd read *The Lives of the Saints*, from which we were to choose and explain our choice of a patron saint. I choose St. Martin of Tours, who in the book's brief description was the first Christian to object on religious grounds to military service. When charged with desertion and cowardice and then jailed, he offered to go into battle unarmed.

I set out from Tours and, after eight weeks of walking and wayside respite through Bordeaux and Burgos, I arrive in Campostello where I sojourn for a week, and then cross over into Portugal and continue walking down the coast to Lisbon to catch a train back to Cherbourg. A little less than halfway, I stop in Porto where I notice banners touting a local museum exhibition of medieval torture devices.

Remembering Father Arthur's tales, I'm curious and go into the local *Museo Soares dos Reis* to see the exhibition and am instantly aghast at the variety of hand-wrought iron objects I could never have imagined, listening to Father Arthur.

Halfway through the exhibit, I leave the museum by a side entrance, fearing I'll be sick. I'm unable to accept their "historic interest" as easily as Father Arthur, who consigns them to Church history and the foibles of men, whereas I retain those haunting images to this day along with the horrors ascribed to each. In my years in the Church, I never saw or experienced sexual abuse but heard often from colleagues that such abuse was widespread. I came to understand that for many sexual predators a religious vocation offered a sanctuary for acting out their sexual fantasies.

And Other Religions

At St, John's, I'm surprised that the curriculum includes the world's great religions: Judaism, Islam, and Buddhism. As taught, the historical chronology makes sense to me. Abraham introduces moral authority and several centuries later influences Yahweism and early Judaism among the Semites. His influence is integral to the formation of Christianity and Islam. Around 500 B.C. the Greeks, seeking answers to their many perceived paradoxes, create all-powerful gods whom they can petition to rationalize their world.

About the same time, in Asia, Siddhartha Gautama, the Buddha, speaks to his apostles of the four noble truths: the perception of suffering, the causes of suffering — desire and ignorance — the end of suffering or *Nirvana*, and the *Noble Path*. Christ, a Jew himself, imbues Abraham's morality with *caritas* — transcendent love, mercy, and compassion.

Five-hundred years later, drawing on the prophets of Christianity and Judaism, Mohammed introduces a spiritual practice in the five pillars: expression of faith, ritual prayer, the giving of alms, fasting during Ramadan, and pilgrimage to Mecca.

A millennium later, Martin Luther uses the moral inconsistencies of Christianity and endemic clerical corruption to justify what will become yet another family of religions.

Paolo and I often discuss our surprise that a Catholic seminary feels comfortable teaching such an array of heresies, remembering

Sister Thérèse telling us in catechism that, although well meaning, our school friends who go to "other churches" will never see the face of God in heaven.

Over the years, I've come to believe that, beyond the teachings of a few earthbound prophets, the invention of new religions or interpretation of old ones has been driven more by human greed, cupidity, and fear than by divine inspiration. On a more hopeful note, I've also come to see how the world's great religions share the same persistent spiritual tenets: forgiveness, mercy, compassion, acceptance, love, humility, and service.

Westover, Vermont

On graduation from St. John's my first assignment is Immaculate Conception parish in Westover, Vermont, a small community of some two thousand souls, about 300 of whom are practicing Catholics. I'm not surprised to learn on my arrival that the parish is struggling with diminishing attendance and collections. I get a modest stipend from the diocese that's augmented by weekly collections for our charitable outreach and parish sustenance. But I've always been accustomed to living within my means, such as they are.

The church has an adjacent pastoral residence, a modular raised ranch. A hand-made 2 x 6 cross adorns the front door. There's no entry handle or stair access to this entrance. Like the reredos behind the church altar, the sealed oak door looks like a framed work of art hung on the façade of the house. The only working entrance is adjacent to a breezeway garage and leads into a cramped kitchen-dining area. There are two bedrooms and a living room-study. The former priest, Father Kincannon, had lived here with his elderly sister. A woman on the parish welcoming committee tells me he died peacefully in his sleep in the master bedroom and the parish finally had to evict his sister from their parish residence.

I retire to my room with its single bed that fills half the floorspace. I unpack and stow my few casual clothes in the closet and dresser, having already put away my few fitted vestments in the wide drawers and closet in the vestry, where I found a full set of chasubles and stoles for the ecclesiastical calendar. I toss my suitcase onto the highest shelf in the closet and then break down the moving boxes that contain my books and a few kitchen utensils my mother pushed on me, knowing I had no idea how to use them. Living in her own past, I suspect she assumes I have a church lady who watches over me, prepares meals, washes my clothes, and cleans house for me — not that I would want that. I relish my solitude even in my loneliness.

I spend the rest of the week settling into my new home and accepting greetings from parishioners who show up at random hours to welcome me and, I suspect, to assess my pastoral skills. The practical realities of my vocation are settling in, and the emotional fortifications I've maintained for so long seem suddenly at risk.

I think of Paolo and his betrayal and wonder if he's been accepted into the Trappists at *Our Lady of Gethsemani*. At our investiture, Paolo hadn't yet been assigned a parish, having asked the Diocesan Office if he might apply to the Cistercian Order of Trappist monks at the *Abbey of Our Lady of Gethsemani* in rural Kentucky. When we parted, he'd heard nothing. He must have found my address from the diocesan o ffice, as I receive a letter from him several weeks after settling in Westover and am thrilled to see his handwriting.

Paolo is living with his estranged aunt in a second-story flat in Rockport, Maine, awaiting an answer from the bishop. His written word reminds me of his spoken voice during our quiet hours together, sharing hopes and fears for our futures in the priesthood. He recounts his efforts to join the cloistered community of Trappists, explaining that they are very selective about whom they accept into their community. He worries that his education won't meet their standards but remains hopeful he'll be accepted. Like me, he's heard that his bishop is under pressure to assign more priests to parishes currently without, and he fears he'll end up like me — assigned to a parish of strangers. Paolo often expressed his discomfort with pastoral duties, preferring instead the monastic life.

As I sit at the white and red Formica kitchen table, reading through the pages of Paolo's beautiful cursive script, his letter becomes more intimate. He writes of his childhood and his father's periodic explosions of anger and violence, how his mother lived in fear of her husband and only intervened on her son's behalf when her husband was too exhausted to leave his chair.

His written voice turns confessional. He apologizes for keeping secrets and goes on to say that he's never felt safe telling anyone who he really is and that I'm the first person in whom he feels he can confide. I've always thought we had no secrets from one another and am both surprised and curious. Our experience as boys growing into men was so similar that in our quiet moments together we spoke openly and unembarrassedly about the conflicts between our sexual misgivings and our desires.

Sipping my tea, I read the last page. Our shared sexual fears and fantasies differ only in one way: Paolo's fantasies are of men.

Suddenly, I feel betrayed and alone. Have our shared moments of fraternal intimacy been just a seduction? I'm alone in a strange and unrecognizable world, our friendship upended. I vow never to write Paolo, a vow that like most, I'll betray in time.

A Confession

It's Saturday afternoon, the posted time for me to hear confessions. Other than my own repetitive confessions of lust and self-abuse and a few concocted venial sins for variety and credibility, I've yet to hear another's confession, offered absolution, or imposed a penance.

I sit alone in the claustrophobic dark of a confessional, flanked on both sides by similar spaces with kneelers for sinners seeking absolution. For the first quarter hour, I'm alone sitting on the clammy Naugahyde bench trying to recall the admonitions of my own childhood priest. In seminary, we were taught to listen carefully, ask questions for clarity, and to then offer advice, absolution, and an appropriate penance.

I hear someone enter the confessional on my left. I wait for them to settle on the kneeler and then slide back the wood panel. The familiar dry sound of the plywood moving in its wooden channel recalls my childhood anxiety about confession. Before I hear her voice, I know from her scent a woman is kneeling next to me. I see only her silhouette as I try and imagine her looks.

"Bless me Father, for I have sinned. My last confession was seven weeks ago. Since then, I've committed mortal sins. I have cheated on my husband again, two times, and lied to him about it. He does not know, but he suspects that I'm being unfaithful. He's too kind to say anything or to confront me directly. He just seems sad and carries on the way he does. It's like he doesn't know how to be angry with me. Something

in me wants him to know and to be furious with me and even hit me, but he is not that kind of man.

"My venial sins pale compared to the mess I've made of my marriage. They're mostly about the lies I tell my family about the secret life I've been living. I donated some clothes to Catholic Charities and put too high a value on them for the tax deduction. I ate meat on Friday one time when I simply forgot at the school cafeteria.

"For these and all the sins I cannot now remember, I ask God's pardon and your absolution, Father."

I realize I've entered an ongoing narrative another priest has heard before me. I'm quiet for a minute and wonder if my shock at hearing her confession was mirrored by the former priest, who had doubtless heard the same confession from others many times before he died.

"Father?"

"Yes, I'm sorry. I'm here. I was just thinking. Did you initiate this sin of the flesh? How long has it been going on?"

"No, father, it happened three years ago, Jim and I were both working late and ran into each other leaving the school. He asked me out for supper and a drink to discuss changes in the school's junior high curriculum and, to our mutual surprise, it just went from there. That was the first time and there've been many more that I confessed to Father Kincannon before you came."

"And how do you plan to stop this marital infidelity, which is an offense against the Sacrament of marriage, your family, and God?"

"That's my real sin, Father. I don't want to end it. He cares about me, and I him. He notices me. He's curious about what I think, how I feel. He's interested in my pleasure, not just his own. I feel like a person when I'm with him."

"Do you have children?"

"No, Leonard and I have had sex only a few times and, despite our desire to have children, our sex has never produced any in our four years together."

"You have committed yourself to this man in the eyes of God. You can neither persist in your sin or walk away from your vows. You must tell me you will end this affair for me to offer absolution."

"I can tell you that, Father, as I did many times to Father Kincannon, but I know it's not true."

"How can I offer you forgiveness if you intend to keep sinning?"

"What should I do, Father? I believe in God and my faith is strong."

"Unless you're willing to renounce this offense to your faith and to God, I can't offer absolution or communion. Pray to the Virgin Mary for her enlightenment and may you come to the right decision for yourself and your husband."

With that, I slide the panel closed and hear her crying softly on the other side. I sit quietly until she stands and leaves. No one's entered the other confessional, so I decide to escape the stale air and go outside until I see someone enter the church.

When I open the confessional door, I see the young woman kneeling at the communion rail, her rosary beads dangling from her left hand. Hearing my footfalls, she turns briefly to see who's there and then turns quickly away, but long enough for me to see her face swollen with tears. The church is empty. I leave by the side door to the vestry. I'd hoped to escape her attention.

Outside, the sun's shining brightly in the cool air that promises an early fall. I gather my cassock and sit on the steps, trying to parse what's just happened in my first confession. I know I failed the young woman still praying in the Church, but I also know I can't offer absolution to one who is so lacking in repentance and is planning to sin again.

I have a sudden instinct to go inside and hold her. The feeling is not sexual. I know I've failed her and myself. I return to the rectory and make a cup of tea. While I wait for the water to boil, I make an *Act of Contrition: "Oh my God, I am heartily sorry for having offended Thee. I detest all my sins because I dread the loss of heaven and the pains of hell. But most of all, because they offend Thee, my God, who are all good and deserving of all my love. I firmly resolve, with the help of Your grace, to sin no more and to avoid temptation, through Christ, Our Lord, Amen."*

The whistle of the kettle returns me to myself. I look out the window to see if there are any cars in the church parking lot and, thankfully, it's empty.

I sit down at the kitchen table with my cup of tea and try to make some sense of my feelings about the young woman whom I've left in the church crying and praying to another woman as I directed. I wanted so much to be held when I was young, a wish rarely indulged by my mother and never by my father. Is that why I imagine this woman might have wanted to be held? Her friend Jim is there for her, even though her remote husband isn't. Is my impulse to hold her in her sadness satisfying a need in her or in me? She came to me for forgiveness and I couldn't give her that. Dispirited, I wonder if the God I want to know is indeed the God I've committed my life to.

I soon adapt to the daily tasks of parish priesthood: hearing confessions on Saturday afternoon and evening, saying Mass daily at seven A.M. for an almost empty church, and again on Sunday at eight and ten A.M.

Gladys Aube, the organist and choirmistress, oversees the small choir of five women and two men who sing at the high Mass on Sunday and at funerals and weddings. Living a few houses down from the church, she attends daily Mass if weather permits. The original Estey Reed pump organ has long since fallen into disrepair and been replaced by a wheezing Kimball organ donated by the local V.F.W. Gladys manages to elicit dreary and erratic accompaniments from it when her choir performs.

The only drama in my days is hearing the sins of others in the gloom of the confessional. Neither life experience nor religious training prepared me for the panoply of sins and intimacies I'm hearing. My childhood fears haunt me even now as I listen to my parishioners describing their sins to me. It dawns on me how little I know of life and how ill-prepared I am to counsel my parishioners. The confusing range of sexual intimacies, experiences, and obsessions I hear are a mystery to me. The playground gossip I heard as a child and the few candid classroom conversations with teachers in seminary never prepared me for what I hear in the confessional. Paolo and I never spoke of such things. I often think about how much I miss Paolo despite his betrayal. I wonder if it was a betrayal at all or just a confidence based in his trust in our friendship.

Another couple comes to the rectory in the afternoon to ask my help in keeping their marriage together. Before coming, they agree to my suggestion that they take turns talking and not interrupt one another as they detail the complaints they see corroding their marriage.

I listen first to the wife talk about her husband's lack of interest in her and about all the time he spends with his pals at the Elks Club. She says she feels alone most of the time and can never manage to engage her husband in a discussion of her loneliness. She says she craves physical contact, not sex so much as a hug, a kiss, and the certainty that what she says and feels matters. Staring at the carpet, she says she feels alone in their marriage.

Her spouse says he feels more connection with his male friends who share his interests, pastimes, stories, and who are just more fun. He admits he feels inadequate when he's with his wife and so spends more and more time away from home. This story will repeat itself many times during my pastoral life.

I develop a routine in which I ask each spouse to recall how and why they came together; what excited them about one another; what survived the initial rush of mystery and desire.

Each recalls a shared moment, skinny-dipping in a quarry the night before their wedding, the birth of their only child, their first new car purchase. The list loses energy as their marital benchmarks turn more material: a house, a camper, a promotion and raise...followed by embarrassed silence.

They look at me or at the floor, but rarely at one another. I urge them to take a few days and go somewhere where they had gone as newlyweds, but I can see their days together are numbered and that one or the other will find solace in another and the sacramental vows of lifelong matrimony will again unwind.

As they leave, I offer them God's blessing in their language...*Que le Dieu vous bénisse et garde*...they nod and thank me as they leave. We both know I haven't helped them. My parishioners come to me wanting the miracles they've been taught are within my reach, but I'm only human and have little capacity for changing their lives, a fact I am coming to understand all too well.

I'm alone again in the parish house. Ordained to believe in my intercessional powers and the eternity of my own promises, I feel my faith weakening, just as the departing couple has lost theirs in me and in one another.

I skip supper and read my breviary before I retire.

A Merry Grig

The priest assigned as my spiritual and parish advisor is a Father Conran in nearby Bennington. The bishop describes Father Conran as a "merry grig" with a full but well-trimmed white beard and a twinkle in his Irish eyes." Father Conran is available to me for questions, and I'm to meet with him monthly to update him on the well-being of my parishioners. As my spiritual advisor, he'll also administer the sacraments to me.

We arrange that I'll drive down on the last Saturday of the month and stay for confessions and his late afternoon Mass. We'll have a bite to eat and then I'll return home to Westover.

At our first meeting, I take an immediate liking to him. He's warm and open and overwhelms me with questions about my upbringing. The fact that I'm French-Canadian and he's Irish matters little to him. This surprises me, as I've come across so many mid-size New England Catholic cities struggling to sustain Irish, French, Italian, and sometimes Polish churches in their communities. The decline in new vocations and in the faithful is forcing diverse cultural communities to consolidate into the last church standing, and some of those have only the benefit of circuit-rider priests. And just as parishioners adjust to worshiping next to Catholics of a different national origin, the bishop presses into service four imported Nigerian priests for some of his vacant parishes.

My anxiety about confessing that I've already broken my commitment to celibacy is unrelieved by Father Conran's warm welcome.

As he enters the center of the confessional, I follow into the right side and kneel. The screen opens immediately, and I hear, "Well…?"

I begin the confessional prayer and then fall silent when it comes time to begin my litany of sins.

"Come, come," Father Conran urges. "Nothing is as bad in the eyes of God as it is in our own. Tell me what you've been up to."

"Bless me, Father, for I have sinned."

I confess to masturbation and skip my usual list of credible venial sins. If I've committed them, I've forgotten them and besides, practically speaking, they don't prevent my entrance into paradise. Again, I go silent.

"Is that all my son?" I hear from the other side of the grill.

"No," I answer. "I've broken my promise of celibacy…with a woman."

"Your first time, I gather?"

"Yes, Father," I answer, unable to call him "Mike," as he has asked.

I recount what I remember, starting with Ellen's confession and ending with my waking up alone and reading her note. I make no effort to diminish my responsibility or to justify it with the sadness and failure I felt after denying her absolution.

"Wonderful tale. You know you did wrong, but it was hardly a willful wrong. You're probably both better for it, especially since it won't happen between you again. 'Passion' is inherent in the word 'compassion.' Think of it, if you can, as mutual absolutions. She has forgiven you for not forgiving her.

"You're coming of age, like us veteran sinners, will make you a better Father-confessor. Funny how satisfying one's self or another became such a sin. I still don't see it, but then again, I didn't invent our list of sins; better behaved men than I did.

"In the eyes of the Church, you've sinned against God. I've no idea who seduced whom, or how the diminished capacity afforded by a healthy dose of Scotch whiskey might play in the eyes of God. As to your self-abuse, I knew an old Boston priest, who each time I confessed masturbation, said, 'Use it or lose it,' I never knew exactly what he meant.

"For your penance, say a Rosary to our Blessed Virgin. She'll understand your sin better than St. Peter. *Ego te absolvo.* "You are forgiven my son, by the God I know and by me. Go and do not sin again. Go in peace and pray to the Virgin for purity of thought and hand. See you inside for a bite and a wee jar after Mass."

With that striking absolution, I leave the confessional, struggling to understand what I've heard. Never in my young years have I heard a priest question the canon of mortal sin or speak to me so casually about mortal sin.

I settle into a pew, say my penance, and sit through the Saturday Mass attended by Catholics with other plans for Sunday. I receive Father Conran's communion which he delivers with a wink.

The rectory attached to St. Boniface matches the 19th-century architecture of the ageing cathedral next to it, reflecting an era when the Church had more wealth and standing. After Mass, I wander down a flagstone path through a rose garden. Father Conran greets departing parishioners on the front steps of the church, after which he'll return to the vestry to put away his vestments. I've no idea what to expect of the man I've just met in the shadows of the confessional.

"Toot-a-loo," I hear behind me and look back up the path to see Father Conran approaching in his cassock.

"Let's have a jar and a bite to eat. Hearing confessions makes me thirsty and ravenous. The body and blood of Christ may replenish the spirit but only aggravate my thirst."

I turn to greet him, and together we walk back to the front door of the rectory and go inside. The dark 19th-century interior reminds me of the interior of the Phillips Estate, and I wonder how Ma's getting on.

"Don't for a minute assume my nifty quarters reflect my lifestyle. The rectory's a relic of an earlier era when the Church had money, real estate, priests, nuns, and an abundance of faithful. Those days are gone, but we get by. I make the three extra bedrooms in here available, as needed, to the local homeless shelter and keep a pot of Irish stew bubbling on the stove. It's the only dish I know how to make, so it's the only food I eat, other than that provided in the transubstantiation. That tiny wafer replenishes the spirit but does little for the body, and the wine…ah, well…the wine. I must be vigilant for that sultry tease! I was an epic drunk and a bit of a satyr with the lasses. It took some face-to-face discussions with a gutter grate for me to finally come to my senses. I now drink *must* instead of that sickly-sweet muscatel most of my brethren use for altar wine. I add lots of water as a defense against alcohol's euphoric evocations. Sometimes during the Consecration, I feel like Tantalus with the grapes and the water just beyond my reach.

"The only escape from my hedonist ways seemed to be the priesthood," he continues, "and it's been a Godsend indeed, though it looks different from the inside than it did from my young days as an altar boy and catechist. My life's manageable now, though I do experience euphoric recall of the sirens I used to bed and the whiskey-sprees I've survived. My own father confessor Father Flanagan was a lush but a wise one, and he used to tell me, 'Liam, St. Peter will judge you not for what occurs to you, as you have no control over that, but for what you do with your thoughts.'" I remembered my own confusion as a young boy about the difference between desire and deed, and which one was a sin.

"You're an onanist…well, aren't we all…celibate men in love with our hands. Did they not teach you that at St. John's? 'Tis a fine school for the priesthood indeed, but they don't prepare us for the world we're entering or, in my case, the world I was leaving.

"Now look, all my malarkey's silenced you. Tell me about you. I know you're from Cabot, went to St. John's seminary, and that you masturbate, but that's all I know."

I take a sip from the glass of port Father Conran hands me and notice he's having tea. Other than the sweet communion wine back in the vestry I use to fill the cruets and my white night with Ellen, I have little experience with alcohol, so I sip the port to give myself a minute to gather myself.

"Unlike you, Father, I'm hardly a man of the world. I entered the priesthood, I think, so I'd never have to be. But as a grownup, almost everything's a surprise to me. I grew up in a working family. My mother's a domestic in a large estate and my father was a stone-cutter before he died of silicosis.

"I knew from a young age, I wanted to be a priest. Father Delaire was our priest. Growing up was scary to me. Unlike my brother, Rosaire, who relished it and now serves in the army, I was afraid a lot. I never hear from him. My sister, aunt, and mother stay in touch. My sister, Lucienne, is going to Marymount College in the fall and Ma will probably retire soon and come live with me."

"Delaire, eh. A *Canuck*, wouldn't've known him. We *Micks* stuck together until things began to fall apart. Now we're all mixed together, *Polacks, Wops, Canucks,* and *Micks,* all men of God.

"You homosexual — not that it matters?"

"No, Father."

"Me neither, never much understood that proclivity, but not up to me to judge God's children."

"My best friend in seminary was though, but he never told me until we parted. He's a Trappist in Kentucky, I think."

"You'll learn that we're all sexual beings, you included. If you remember it, you've now had the experience of physically loving another human being. That will help inform the next forty years of pastoral counselling you'll dispense to couples struggling with their own relationships.

"I know...I shouldn't say such things, but celibacy's a Church invention. I don't have sex anymore; had my share of it when I was young. I still "abuse myself" as the prurient nuns like to say — what few there are left. I suspect they do, too. But as Father Flanagan used to say, 'You won't burn in hell for what you think, only for what you do, and self-love is hardly evil. It's natural. Happens all the time in the animal kingdom from which we're descended.

"Don't quote me to the bishop, who's a prude and doesn't cotton much to evolution."

I'm at a loss and take another sip of port.

"Let me fetch you a bowl of my stew. After 35 years, it just gets better and better."

With that, Father Conran disappears through a doorway. I'm grateful to be alone and for the sudden quiet.

Father Conran bustles back in bearing a tray with two large bowls of steaming stew and a plate with several buttered slices of soda bread. He places the tray on a vitrine coffee table displaying a collection of antique rosary beads. He passes me a bowl and a spoon and urges me to try his stew.

"It's delicious." I venture.

"One of the church biddies bakes me this wonderful soda bread from a recipe from the old sod and brings it to Mass every Sunday. Reminds me of home.

"I know you've got to get on the road, but please know I'm here to help and shall welcome your visit at the end of next month. I know it all must seem strange to you, being a new pastor, but it will come to make sense. Give it time. What you didn't learn in life about human behavior, you'll learn in the confessional. We're all fallible and therein lies our beauty and promise. Now, go in peace, and I'll see you next month. Let me give you my blessing."

I kneel on the ornate carpet and hear Father Conran intone: *In nomine Patris, et Filii et Spiritus Sancti, Amen.*

I stand up, accept his warm hug, thank him, and walk to my car. It's getting dark. I turn on the headlights and welcome the drive home with only the monotony of road noise.

Ellen and Jimmy

My morning goes quickly. I enjoy the new altar boys in training. One is quiet. His reticence and deference remind me of myself at his age; the other's an outgoing character, finding humor in the staid choreography of serving Mass and the feminine flounce of his crisp white surplice. He reminds me of the boys I found threatening when I was young. But the threat's gone, and I'm able to admire his sense of himself. How could I have known so little of myself?

I withdraw the confessional slide and a silhouette of the woman I heard in my first confession appears in the shadows. Only when I hear her voice (which seems lower now) do I recognize Ellen.

She dispenses with the formalities of confession and says in a slow alto, *"Father Pierre, it's me, Ellen. You probably don't want to talk to me after what happened. You wouldn't give me absolution last time I came to confession since I couldn't promise you I'd never sin again in that same way, but you did later when we were together. I've sinned again.*

I'm leaving Leonard and will tell him in the next few days. He'll be relieved. He'll protest, saying he loves me and that he needs me. He's a rational man and knows that love and need are integral to a marriage. He'll miss my presence in his life, but not the intimacy I've pressed on him since our early days together. Above all, he needs surety and I've deprived him of that. I'm not angry at him but have chosen not to live alone in a marriage. The man I'm going to loves me and wants me.

"After I came to the rectory and we talked, I felt we understood one another, even as I knew our religion would never allow you to offer me absolution, but you did. Even if you hadn't, I thought our act of love was a form of absolution if only personal, an expression of your compassion, and I will be forever grateful for the tenderness you showed me.

"I know others are waiting for confession, so I must ask you. 'Is my life in the Church over? Since I can't receive the sacraments as a divorced woman. Do I pack up my childhood faith and leave? As a man of God, do you think we make our own heaven, purgatory, or hell on earth or does that rest solely with God's judgment in the afterworld?"

I'm at a loss for how to answer.

"Go in peace," I answer under my breath and close the slide in panic. I give myself a minute before opening the other slide. My inability to answer Ellen's question betrays my understanding of the life of Christ who both loved and forgave sinners. What is so broken in me or my Church that am I at such a loss for how to answer her?

I hear several more perfunctory confessions and offer similarly perfunctory penances. Many of the older parishioners seem to labor to find enough sins to make their habitual confessions. Rarely do I hear a mortal sin from them, but they leave my confessional pleased with another clean slate, the ability to receive communion, and a passport to paradise when they die.

I open the slide on the other side and a young man intones the opening to confession, *"Bless me, Father, for I have sinned... ."*

He confesses the regular sins of young men: dirty thoughts, masturbation, and the litany of venial sins that begin to sound as if all young boys share a common inventory.

"Is that all, my son?" I ask after a prolonged silence.

"No, Father, I don't want to live any longer."

"What do you mean?" I ask, not sure I heard his whispered response.

"I just don't want to be alive any more. I don't have any friends. I'm not good at anything like sports or studies. Kids pay no attention to me. They don't even care enough to tease me. It's like I'm not there."

"Are you saying you want to end your life?"

"Yes, but I don't know how, and you'll tell me it's a mortal sin and that if I die with a mortal sin on my soul, I'll go to hell forever. I know all that; I'm just tired of living this way."

I'm silent. Again, I have no idea how to respond. I can't seek professional help for him, as that would break the bonds of confession. He and I both know that trying to dissuade him with threats of hellfire and eternal damnation mean little.

"Have you spoken to your parents or a doctor about this?" I ask.

"I'm talking to you about it. I don't really have anyone else to talk to about it. My foster parents are kind people, but they don't know me. They feed me and see to my needs, but otherwise they shy away from me. They never had kids of their own and fostered me when Mr. Halverson retired from his job. I wouldn't want to hurt or scare them. They're kind people.

"At school, I spend my time either in the classroom or study hall. I've never been a sports kid. Like others who hate gym, I'm in what the kids call spaz class. I don't even like school. I never get sick, so I've never been to a doctor, except to have a wart burned off my foot when I was twelve."

"Don't think of suicide as a sin; think of it as an offense against God," I say.

"I don't know God," he answers.

"God knows you," I say half-heartedly.

"How would I know? I went to catechism because my fosters are Catholic and raised me that way. I don't know any God and, if there is one, I doubt he knows me."

I want to tell him my name, offer some connection through the grill that separates us, and I ask him his name. He answers, *"Jimmy."* I then hear him stand up and leave.

Again, I'm at a loss. Did he want absolution for a sin he was thinking of committing? Did he want me to intervene? Can I help him and not violate the bounds of confession?

Two of my confessions have ended with the penitents walking out. I hear seven more confessions, but my mind keeps returning to Jimmy. His loneliness recalls my own, though I never imagined ending my life, only sheltering it. Was his sadness the result of his loneliness or the cause of it?

Shouldn't I intervene? What if Jimmy were to act on his impulse? I vow to find him. His foster parents must be in the parish records, but I didn't get a last name. Besides, Jimmy's last name wouldn't necessarily be the same as his foster parents'.

I hear five more confessions, sins mumbled with varying degrees of sincerity. Many seem like the inevitable transgressions of half-lived lives. A young boy repeats verbatim my weekly childhood confession of self-abuse and adds the rote mix of venial sins. Recalling a question I once heard in seminary, I ask him if he knows the difference between "self-abuse" and "a nocturnal emission." There's a long silence, and I realize he has no idea what I'm talking about. I whisper, "a wet dream," eliciting a confused silence. I can see through the grate that he's looking down rather than at me.

Flustered, I explain to him the difference between purposeful masturbation and the involuntary act that often results from a dream of sexual stimulation. But I've only succeeded in confusing and embarrassing him. The distinction's beyond his ken as are the prerequisites of sin: understanding and willfulness, which we parsed so logically as seminarians. I've only succeeded in distancing him from the relief and grace of his labored confession. I offer absolution and ten Hail Marys as penance. The church is empty now and I return to the rectory.

I receive little mail at my new address, but out of habit check the rusty mailbox near my driveway. I recognize the handwriting on the letter I find in there; the return address: *Fra Paolo Barza, Cistercian Order of Trappists, Abbey of Our Lady of Gethsemani, Bardstown, Kentucky.* I remember with amusement how we addressed one another as "Fra…"

I go into the rectory and pour myself a tumbler of wine from a bottle of Almaden red a parishioner dropped off as a welcome gift. I've yet to recover any taste for Scotch and, other than the wine used in the Mass during the Consecration, I have no experience with wine and am, at first, put off by its tannic bitterness. I set the glass down and open the trifold pages and begin reading.

> *Fra Pierre,*
>
> *As you can see, I was accepted and am now happily installed as a postulant in the Trappist order at the Our Lady of Gethsemani Abbey. I have never been so happy and often find myself remembering our many discussions together.*
>
> *I hope you understood my telling you that I'm a homosexual. I never contemplated any relationship with you other than the one we enjoyed for so long during our time as seminarians.*
>
> *Like you, I'm committed to my vows of celibacy, and the fact that I was born homosexual doesn't compromise my faith. With the help of my confessor, I try to understand the Church's tenet making homosexuality a sin.*

Are my natural inclinations a sin, or is it only the practice of them? I may never know. Being born with a sexual attraction to men was hardly a choice. But my decision to remain celibate is, and I hope that it vindicates any sin of my birth in the eyes of God if not the Church. It's a discussion I have with my confessor here in the Abbey. He's not a homosexual but knows and counsels without judgment many brothers who are.

He believes we are all born on a spectrum of sexuality between homosexual and heterosexual desire and that our place in that spectrum can change during our lives. When I heard him say that, I remembered being overwhelmed by my niece's entrance into puberty and the many nights I would lie in bed trying to imagine what was happening underneath the pinafores she always wore when my aunt and uncle came to visit us on certain saint days or for the blessing of the fleet.

Brother Dominic reminds us that God only holds us accountable for what we do, not what we imagine or dream. I am finally and gratefully comfortable with that knowledge today.

I hope you are well and happy and fulfilled in your new parish. I so valued our time together in seminary and the quiet time it gave me to think and pray that I have committed my time on this earth to our monastic community where I'm learning to be a baker.

I can only pray to God that you receive my letter in the spirit in which I send it. I ask God's and your forgiveness for any misunderstanding.

Fraternitas in nomine Patris, et Filii, et Spiritus Sancti.

Paolo

Shaken, I pour myself another glass of wine, get a box of Saltines from the cupboard, and go into the living room to sit in my one comfortable chair. I read Paolo's letter several times and finish two more glasses of wine and a wax-paper column of crackers.

Looking out the window at the waning light, I think of our many times together after vespers. Facing the window, I see a fine mist of dry dust that seems to hang in my livingroom air, made visible only in the fading slant of western light. I refold the letter and insert it back into its envelope.

The slant of dust-infused light brings back a memory from my first year of catechism. Sister Thérèse told us that the brilliant late afternoon light that often succeeds a heavy storm and looks like a glowing staircase to heaven means that a child somewhere on earth has died, and God has sent an angel down to earth to lead the child into heaven. It was the first time I'd heard that children could die like their grandparents, and I was afraid and wondered why God would take a child.

More and more, my choice of vocation seems to reflect my youthful cowardice. I thought I'd be safe nestled in the bucolic, celibate life of a parish priest. But now I've slept with a woman seeking God's forgiveness and I had no answers for a boy who just confessed his desire to end his life. How did I come to know so little of life?

I stand up and feel my first sense of intoxication. It feels good, a palliative for my persistent self-doubt. I crumple up the loud wax paper, toss it into the sink, and go to bed where I read my breviary, say my prayers, and resolve to write Paolo in the morning after Mass.

Although I think of him daily, months go by before I write. I'm still trying to reconcile his place in the Church with its teaching on homosexuality. Have I betrayed my only real friend as I have two of my parishioners?

A busy schedule distracts me from my shortcomings: writing homilies, saying daily Mass for the two or three faithful who attend, funerals, marriages, counseling, catechism, and visiting the sick in nearby Windsor Hospital. I am also beginning to make regular visits to Windsor Prison at the request of the warden to see prisoners asking for counsel or the sacraments.

Among my pastoral duties, I'm least prepared for hearing confessions. When I enter the confessional, I feel like I'm entering a dark theater with no idea what will be projected on the screen. My seminary training focused on clarity and rectitude and defining the very nature of sin. I was taught little of the sinner's need for connection, forgiveness, and compassion.

Other than Ma, Lucienne, and my friendship with Paolo, I've managed to distance myself from anyone eliciting feeling in me. Was this my father's endowment who could ping pong between verbal rage and sullen silence? Ellen and Paolo want to be loved and valued. Am I somehow different?

I suddenly feel very calm and fall into a deep sleep until my alarm wakes me in time for seven o'clock Mass.

After Mass, I return to the rectory and make myself a bowl of instant oatmeal on the unfamiliar electric stove. I slice a banana into the stained Melamine bowl with its web of hairline cracks and add a mixture of cinnamon and sugar as Ma used to do. I pour a mug of hot coffee from the electric percolator I'd set before saying Mass for the only person in church, Gladys Aube.

I note from the burn stains along the chrome perimeter of the Formica table that my predecessor smoked. I suddenly notice burn-rings and arcs here and there on the table where hot pans were set down without trivets or hot pads.

Rosaire

As I finish my cooling oatmeal, staring at the halo-shaped burns, wondering what Ma would think of such carelessness, the phone rings. It's Ma crying uncontrollably. She wants to come and see me today.

"Ma, what's wrong?" I ask into her sobs.

"I have to tell you in person. There's a bus at 11:15 that gets in a 2:30. Can you meet me? It stops at the Rexall in Westover."

"Ma, tell me what's happened. Have you been fired? Are Lucienne and Rosaire okay? What's going on? I've never heard you like this. Is Jeanine sick? Tell me, and yes, of course, come today."

In my anxiety, I realize I'm pressing the heavy Bakelite receiver too hard against my ear. It hurts. Trying to imagine what news has reduced Ma to tears, I relax my arm, as Ma sobs her way back to words. I don't ever remember hearing fear in her voice. If she ever knew fear, she kept it from us as children. Nor have I ever heard her lose herself in sadness, even the day Pa died. His slow decline afforded us time to adjust to the inevitability of his death, to accompany him in his dying as much as he'd let us, and to understand that, this time, he was leaving us for good.

After a brief silence, Ma resumes, "Two uniformed soldiers came to the door, and I knew right away. I said, 'Is Rosaire hurt?'

"One of the soldiers stepped forward and took my forearm and the other said, 'Rosaire died in action, Ma'am. As you know, he was with the 23rd infantry regiment and died a hero's death on or about September 22nd fighting the Korean People's Army. We are so sorry to tell you this. You will receive an official letter shortly confirming his death in the service of his country along with any details that are known of his death. Is there a family member nearby who can be with you?'

"I thanked them both for their kindness. They seemed so young themselves. I could only imagine how hard their job must be, telling families of the death of their sons, fathers, and brothers.

"They asked if there was anything more they could do to help me. I managed a smile for their kindness and thanked them, assuring them they'd been very kind. They did a military about-face and walked down the steps, returning to the dark car they'd come in. I just stood there staring after them."

I meet Ma at the Rexall. The bus is a half-hour late, so I have time alone in my car to think about what to say to her.

The pea-green Rambler American I bought used when I came to Westover had also been owned by a smoker and the inside upholstery is rank with the smell of stale tobacco, so I often drive with the windows down unless it's too cold or raining. Corrosion around the car's exterior wheel wells and running boards placed the car comfortably in my price range. Rosaire lent me $200 of the $350 I paid for it, and as I sit on the stained plastic-weave bench seat of the car anxious about Ma's arrival, it occurs to me I'll never have to pay him back.

The bus rolls up and only Ma gets out. I'm standing there to greet her and put my arms around her, as she starts crying again.

"I still can't believe it. He was so young. Elise DuRocher's son also died this week. She just called me last weekend. I don't understand what they're fighting for half-way around the world. I try to follow the news on the radio, but still can't understand why our boys are being sent half way 'round the world to fight and die. For what? They say to prevent Communism, but there's no Communist threat on our borders. Sometimes I think Rosaire was too brave and too ready to fight. Your Pépère was the same way 'til he got the breathing sickness."

"Ma, let's go back to the rectory where we can talk. I can't believe Rosaire's gone."

"He's not gone, Pierre; he's dead. You must know there's a difference."

"I'm sorry, Ma. It just hasn't settled in yet."

I carry Ma's small overnight bag in and set it on the kitchen floor. She's still gathering herself but can't resist inspecting my new quarters.

"This is a nice home or was when it was built, but whoever's been living here wasn't much of a housekeeper. Do you have someone who comes in and cleans from time to time?"

"No, Ma, the parish doesn't have any resources for help and no one's offered. I manage well enough."

I put Ma's bag in the guest room and then return to put a kettle on for tea.

"Let's go sit in the living room. I still can't believe it. Didn't they say anything else about how he died?"

"I don't think they know. Their job's simply to inform families of the death. They said the letter would tell us whatever they know. But I mean, what else is there to know in a war? They tell everyone their son died a hero's death, serving his country, but what does that mean about how he died on the other side of the earth without any of his family to be with him. Was it slow? Was it sudden? Was he alone?"

Ma begins sobbing again. I go into the kitchen to fetch tea for us. I've never been good at emotions, anyone else's, much less my own, and I've no idea how to understand or react to Rosaire's death. We weren't close. He was always stronger and more confident. Unlike me, maturity came naturally to him. He was good to me, but I always felt less somehow, though he never said I was.

I set two cups of tea down on the mahogany coffee table in front of the couch. With her slender finger, Ma traces another burn mark in the mahogany.

"Shameful and careless… such nice furniture once! The priest who lived here didn't pay much attention to his worldly goods. I hope he took better care of his soul and the souls of his parishioners than he did of his home and furniture."

Ma and I talk for the rest of the afternoon, punctuated by her occasional relapse into tears. I try to maintain a sad demeanor but feel only a vacancy. I realize I had more feelings for Rosaire alive than I do now and feel guilty about my inability to absorb the fact that he's dead.

Jeanine calls around five o'clock, having gotten Ma's note asking her to call her at my house. Ma tells her the news and begins crying softly into the phone. I can hear Jeanine's voice through the receiver like some distant shortwave voice. She, too, is crying. I leave Ma and Jeanine to talk and go into the kitchen to make us some supper.

I know little about food. Ma saw to home and hearth, sharing her domestic knowledge only with Lucienne. I guess she thought Rosaire and I would marry housekeepers.

The only food I know how to make other than sandwiches and oatmeal comes from cans. Tonight, I make my signature dish, *tuna-pea wiggle*, as Ma used to call it. I open and pour into an aluminum sauce pan a can each of tuna, boiled peas, and Campbell's mushroom soup. I heat it, stirring it so it doesn't burn on the bottom of the pan, and serve it when it's hot. I like it and make it often for myself.

I go into the living room, where Ma's leaning back on the couch, staring outdoors at a darkening sky. This late afternoon light again recalls vespers, but I hear nothing.

"Does Lucienne know?" I ask.

"Jeanine's going to tell her when she gets home from work," Ma answers. "I feel like I should be there, but there's no bus back until tomorrow late morning. I know she'll be heartbroken, too. She's leaving for Marymount in a month, and she'll be all alone there with no family around."

I switch on the brass floor lamp next to my chair flooding the small living room with a garish white light and invite Ma into the kitchen for supper. I set the table with the stained Melamine dishes and nickel silver restaurant-ware that came with my kitchen. Ma removes some hardened egg yolk from a prior meal she sees between the tines of her fork with her thumbnail, wiping it on her paper napkin, but says nothing. I pretend not to notice. After a few bites, she compliments me on my casserole.

We clear and wash the dishes. Ma makes us some cocoa from a yellow box she finds in the cupboard, and we settle back into the living room. Neither of us has anything left to say. Ma's exhausted from crying and from her trip. My facial muscles ache from sustaining a sad demeanor all day. We hold one another briefly and retire to our rooms.

Three weeks later, when a small honor guard delivers Rosaire's remains in a flag-draped casket to the Ferland Funeral Home, I drive my Rambler home, billowing smoke, to officiate at a funeral Mass in my childhood church. I'm grateful to find a new priest there, Father Estey, about whom Ma had had good words in her weekly letter. It's my first Mass for the Dead. "The dead," I remember, is my own brother as I pull on a black chasuble. I still feel like an altar boy in this church, so rife with childhood memories. Many of the faces in the pews are familiar and I greet and accept the condolences of all those that elicit a name as well as those that don't.

After the Mass, Rosaire is buried at Ste. Anne's cemetery four blocks from the church. Ma, Jeanine, Lucienne, and I stand next to one another. Lucienne and I hold hands and say nothing, only stepping forward after taps is played and the flag has been removed from the casket, folded diagonally, and handed over to Ma. We each lay a small bouquet of flowers on the casket and retreat to our place overlooking the dark rectangular hole in the earth into which Rosaire is being lowered by six bearers. I see again in my mind the hole in Hope Cemetery into which Pa's colleagues lowered him. I wonder if Rosaire is more Pa's son than I am. Ma is crying. Jeanine comforts her. Lucienne is looking away.

After the service, we return to the house on Congress Street where Mrs. Phillips has ordered a catered luncheon for those who come by after the burial. Her affection for Ma is reflected in the food laid out on a white-linen-covered folding table in our living room. There are three *tortières,* a large platter of open-faced cucumber and egg-mayonnaise sandwiches with the crusts removed, and a trencher of gravy-soaked poutine. Given the Phillipses' aversion to spirits, I'm surprised to see an ice bucket full of beer and two bottles of Seagram's *Crown Royal* whiskey standing amid a parade formation of short and long glasses. A young girl, wearing the same white and red-trimmed lace apron over a dark skirt, reminds me of Ma when she was young, and sees that everyone is served and replenishes the table as needed.

Looking at the guests standing around talking in whispers and holding plates of food and glasses, I realize I know none of Rosaire's friends. I recognize a few of Ma's friends, and I see Mrs. Phillips sitting quietly in our ratty armchair by herself.

When the guests leave, and the caterers have packed up the remaining food and stowed it in our fridge, Ma, Lucienne, Jeanine, and I sit down at the kitchen table, relieved to be alone again. Lucienne says a few words about how nice the service was and how kind it was of Mrs. Phillips to have put on such a lovely feed for the guests. Ma smiles and Lucienne begins to cry softly. Jeanine comforts her while Ma fetches us all cups of tea from the teapot warming on the stove. We're talked and cried out, as the realization of Rosaire's permanent absence in our lives settles in.

I leave around nine and get home just after midnight. After morning Mass, I must prepare my Sunday sermon, hear confessions in the afternoon, and oversee an older altar boy who's training two new altar boys to serve Mass. On the way home, I try to imagine Rosaire navigating an afterlife. I recall Sister Thérèse's image of a dead person's ascension through clouds on a staircase of light, and St. Peter's imposing iron gate. It all seems illusory.

Windsor Prison

Ma calls today. Hearing her voice, I'm ashamed. I haven't called her to ask how she's managing. She asks me how I'm doing, and I realize she wants me to help her remember Rosaire. She says she's calling to see if I want any of the things in Rosaire's room. She's cleaning out our room to make space for a boarder. With Lucienne away, it's just her and Jeanine, and they can use the extra income.

I try to remember our room, which contained mostly Rosaire's things — sports items, pennants, a few racy calendar girls, a football, the .22 rifle of which Rosaire was so proud, his open-ended wrench set that Pa gave him when he was twelve, and a Ruger pistol he loved to fire at cans in the backyard before he joined up. I realize there were very few traces of my presence in our room except the plastic crucifix over my bed that absorbed daylight and radiated it back at night. Was I so devoid of interests? I tell Ma she can give away anything she finds in our room.

"I took that military portrait of Rosaire in uniform to a local shop to have two more prints made and framed for you and Lucienne. I knew you'd want one," she says.

"Thank you, Ma, I do, and I'll get it when I next come."

"When will that be?" she asks.

"How about I come for your birthday next month?"

"That would be lovely. I'd like that. Do you think often of Rosaire?"

"I do, and I pray for him," I lie, not knowing why. I hardly ever think of him. Am I so selfish, so inured to, or afraid of, how I might feel?

After lunch, I get another call from the warden at Windsor Prison asking me to return to see a few Catholic boys who've requested confession and communion. I agree, and we set a date for the following afternoon.

Leaving after an early lunch to make the forty-five-minute drive from Westover to Windsor, I'm relieved to be out of the rectory, which I find increasingly depressing.

My dreary thoughts are relieved by the rural landscape as I pass farms and small houses where normal people live and make their ways in life.

Approaching the security gate, I remember I'm pre-cleared and am waved through by the guard noting my license number the warden requested on his call. Driving up the long access road, I'm again daunted by the immense farm housing a hundred men in small cages. I feel like Dante entering hell with no Virgil to guide me.

From what I've learned in my few months of prison ministry, I know that justice can be quixotic. The few men I've met and counselled since moving to Westover have rarely had the benefit of adequate legal counsel or have waived their right to an attorney and represented themselves. Some accepted plea bargains only to think better of it in later years. Still others pleaded guilty to crimes they didn't commit when told by their lawyer that they would lose if their case went to a jury.

I'm early and park in the visitors lot. My mind wanders to the difference between canon and civil law, celestial and terrestrial justice. Consignment to hell or purgatory seems to me more a matter of circumstance and timing than intent and commission. The Church's sale of plenary indulgences in the Medieval and Renaissance eras mirrors for me the contemporary injustice I see for the prisoners I counsel who can't afford legal representation. I remember Paolo joking about a "contingent act of contrition" if he were to have a serious accident. An *act of perfect contrition* may substitute for a full confession, sparing the penitent hell-fire and securing him passage into purgatory.

Today, if a dying sinner has access to confession, receives absolution, and says penance before dying, he'll go to purgatory to atone for his sins, whereas dying unexpectedly with a mortal sin on one's soul consigns one eternally to hell. When I was a child, the distinction seemed arbitrary to me but ensured my weekly confession. But then I'd also assumed grown-ups didn't masturbate and children didn't die.

For unbaptized infants, Sister Thérèse taught us that their consignment to limbo was the same as heaven but without God, which didn't seem so bad. I remember thinking that being in the presence of God the Father would be a terrifying experience.

As time went on, my childhood fears were less about burning in the fires of hell than about eternity. When Lucienne once asked Sister Thérèse how long eternity lasted, she answered with a parable about a sparrow on a beach on earth. The sparrow picks up one grain of sand in its beak and flies it to the moon and then returns for another until he has moved the entire beach to the moon. Then he reverses his flights until he has moved the beach from the moon back to earth. He moves the beach back and forth between earth and the moon as many times as there are grains of sand.

Life on earth was not all that easy and living for that length of time was more terrifying to me than the heat of hell. I could only imagine how the many lifers inside the prison must have felt.

At the appointed hour, I leave my car in the lot and go to the visitors entrance where I'm also expected. A guard ushers me through several slamming steel gates and by a visitor briefing and waiting area into the low-security unit's assembly room, where about a dozen men sit in folding chairs chatting with one another. The guard introduces me only as "Father Pierre" and leaves.

I greet the men, whose attention I now have, and tell them a bit about my background. I'm asked a light-hearted question about my own run-ins with the law and come up empty, admitting I was too afraid as a child to do much wrong. This elicits a few laughs and some knowing smiles. I ask the crowd what landed them in prison and half the hands go up.

An older man says he's serving the last decade of a twenty-year sentence for multiple robberies. He freely acknowledges his guilt, explaining that his mother began drinking after his father died in the war. The V.A. benefits barely covered the cost of their two-story walk-up in a rough section of Glens Falls. At fifteen, he dropped out of school and tried to get a job to supplement their V.A. check but was told he was too young for full-time employment. He began shoplifting at the local grocery store with considerable success but was later caught and got off with a reprimand.

His mother's descent into catatonic alcoholism, and the various boyfriends frequenting their apartment for a free meal, turned him to robbing untended tills in small retail stores, soon escalating to armed robberies of gas station on the outskirts of town. He enjoyed the anonymous notoriety and soon became addicted to the adrenalin high of pursuit and escape until he was finally caught in a set-up and remanded to Windsor to serve out his sentence.

I ask what he plans to do when he gets out.

"Ma's dead and I have no place or family to go home to. This here's my home. I'd rather just stay here, but they won't let me. I have no job, no education, and no work experience other than criminal. Maybe I can get a job in construction. I dunno."

I call on another younger man who breathlessly relates the injustice of his charge of child sexual abuse.

"We 'as in love. She 'as only sixteen and I 'as twenty-one but we loved each other and was plannin' ta git married. Her parents made her lie that I'd raped her and when she went on the stand, she broke down and said she loved me and admitted we was gittin' married, but the law went against me and sided with her parents and I got fifteen years and won't never be allowed to live or work anywhere since I'se known as a "sex offender," which ain't true. I never fucked anybody who di'n't want me ta. I ain' that kind a' guy. I guess this jail's gonna be my home. Not so bad if'n ya' don't mind gettin' fucked in the ass ever' week. First words I heard comin' in was, 'Either I get shit on my dick or blood on my knife… yer choice.'"

I hang my head, not knowing what to say. I can see the men looking at their feet and grinning at my embarrassment. I've heard a few of these words individually before but never in casual conversation or sequenced in a way that conveys such horror. I can't conceive of the sex described. Much later, I wonder if that's what Paolo envisaged in love, not violence.

I call on one more resident, explaining that I'll hear confessions and offer communion in the chapel right afterwards.

A man in his seventies announces he's a "lifer" and plans to die here. I ask if he has family outside.

"Yeah, I got two daughters. One's been tryin' to get me out on somepin' called "compassion release" 'cause a' my age 'n' all, but the prison and p'role officers, say there ain't no such thing, and I gotta serve my sentence. I killed my wife when the girls was little and got a life sentence for it. She 'as always fuckin' 'round with other men, even some a' the guys I worked with at the printing plant.

"I deserved it, but then the girls got fostered out to some creep who messed with them when they was only kids. I felt hopeless, couldn't do nothin' in here.

Wanted to kill the bastard and said so to the parole board. After that, I never heard from them again. Truth is… I'd kill the bastard today if'n I could.

"My girls stopped coming to visit me 'bout fifteen years back. Must be middle-age women now, if they'se even 'live. I know what that kind of kiddy-diddling can do to a youngster. I seen it with my cousin. She ate herself to death and died of the sugar at 42. Must a' weighed 300 hundred pounds when she died. Made damn sure no one'd ever wanna have sex with 'er again."

I thank the men and promise to return. We're escorted into the nearby chapel where a confessional has been set up behind a screen with a chair for me and a prie-dieu next to it. I hear a dozen short confessions; almost all the sins are single-sex sins or involve outbursts of physical violence for which the penitents don't seem that contrite. I hear no venial sins. I dole out penances, offer the men absolution, and then serve communion to those still there.

The guard, who's been sitting through both our meeting in the assembly room and my administration of the sacraments, then sends the men back to their cells and escorts me into another wing some distance away, the high-security unit.

In here, there's no common assembly. Convicts are brought in one at a time to the visiting area, behind a half-inch thick, plate-glass partition. A small, round grill allows for two-way speech but not the passing of any objects. I'm positioned on the visitor side of one section, and the handcuffed men are brought in on the other side. I hear their confessions. I'm limited to five minutes per prisoner, so there's little chance for questions or counselling. Several of the "confessions" are actually desperately whispered pleas for legal help from unresponsive lawyers, urgent messages to family members who've gone silent, or other requests for my help. I feel powerless.

Two men ask for communion, which I serve, one at a time. Then I'm guided to the visitor exit and hear the gate slam shut behind me. On the way home, I remember Jimmy's subdued tenor speaking haltingly in confession of his invisibility, loneliness, and isolation.

Paolo Barza

I know the rectory will be cold when I get home since I've taken to turning the thermostats down when I leave to save on electricity, so I stop at a diner halfway home and have the blue plate special — fried chicken with gravy, fries and sugary coleslaw. When the young waitress sets my plate in front of me with a smile, I glance up at the shallow décolletage formed by her young breasts, hoping to camouflage my interest with a "thank you" after she takes my order.

When I get home, I turn up the thermostat controlling the electric baseboard in my bedroom. Within a few minutes, I smell the accumulated dust borne up into the room by the rise of dry heat. I sneeze several times, pour myself a glass of wine, and lie back in bed, still in my cassock, collar, and black shoes.

I think again how unprepared I am for the life I've chosen, how little I understand of my parishioners' confessions, learning about their lives vicariously in the shadows of the confessional, trying to imagine their sins. I can barely recall the details of my own sin against my celibacy. I remember I'm due at Father Conran's next week for my parish report and monthly sacraments.

As I lie in bed and the wine dulls my effort to read and follow the office lesson for the day, I set the black leather breviary on the bedstead. Out of the blue, a chapel conversation I'd had with Paolo one morning comes to me. We were discussing the Jesuitical arguments we'd just heard in a debate between adherents of liberation theology as derived from a study of the life of Christ and the Vatican's doctrinal interpretation of New and Old Testament teachings on morality. We agreed that Christ's life as portrayed in the gospels was difficult to reconcile with Church teaching. The paradox still haunts me as I listen to and contemplate sins of which I could never conceive. How will I ever know to use my powers of absolution wisely?

Paolo reminded me how, in medieval times, the Church's dogmatism and greed for wealth and power led to the lucrative sales of indulgences — the spark igniting Martin Luther's Protestant revolution.

The next morning, I celebrate Mass with, and for, one lone altar boy. I return to the rectory for a breakfast of instant oatmeal and coffee, both brought to life by a kettle of boiling water. The phone rings. It's Ma. She's filled with news about how well Lucienne's doing at Marymount, preparing to teach grade school when she graduates. Jeanine, too, is well, and my fears of more bad news are unfounded. Ma volunteers little about herself, hoping, no doubt, I will ask, which I do.

"I'm fine," she reports. I'll probably retire next year. Mr. and Mrs. Phillips are going to downsize and move into their summer house on the shore in Newport, Rhode Island. It's smaller and more to their scale as they get older. They won't need as many domestics. They've not yet said anything, but there's talk in Montpelier of them turning the estate into a museum like the Hildene House in southern Vermont we visited many years ago."

Ma rambles on with more local news. I ask her again if she's feeling okay and she admits to some arthritis in her hands, arms, and neck, but assures me that otherwise she's fine. She adds that she's taken to writing things down and making lists to make up for her aging memory. I ask about her and Jeanine's finances and, again, she assures me that they're doing fine between their two salaries and the rental income from Jeanine and Morris's former home. She tells me she's sold her car, as they're within walking distance of everything they need downtown, and a new local jitney service means they can both ride to and from work daily without the expense of maintaining an old car and buying gas.

We talk for a few more minutes. She asks me how I'm doing and how I'm adjusting to the priesthood, if I've gotten to know some folks in my parish, and if I'm eating well. She asks again if I have a cleaning lady yet to help with the chores and keep the rectory clean. I answer in the positive to everything except the cleaning lady, flattering her with the notion that she taught me well, and I can manage keeping my own house clean while staying abreast of my pastoral duties. I make a mental note to clean up thoroughly before her next visit, during which she will sneak her usual finger-swipes for dust accumulation. Sometime in the night, I must have shed my priestly garb, as I wake up beneath the covers at 5:30 A.M. in my undershirt and shorts.

I have a morning funeral Mass and interment and get home from the cemetery and family gathering in the deceased's home around 3:15. I check the rusty mailbox that rarely contains anything more than supermarket fliers and a monthly ecclesiastical supply catalog. There's a letter inside and an electric bill. I recognize the ivory colored paper, the lengthy return address, and Paolo's elegant handwriting. I'm ashamed. I've again broken a promise to myself to write Paolo and remember how much he is still with me.

Dear Brother Pierre,

I cannot tell you how happy I am to be here. I have found my place in the world and, by all accounts, am excelling in the art of breadmaking.

My brothers congratulate me on my loaves, of which I have several specialties. I make a black Russian rye that's become very popular. The brothers like it with sour cream and trout they catch and smoke from our local stream. I also make a very good sourdough baguette that is popular. My own favorite is a very dense seeded rye. My fans tell me two slices, slathered with our hand-churned butter and a dash of salt, makes a meal in itself. But, alas, I didn't write you to bore you with my baking skills.

I hope you are well. My favorite part of living among fellow Trappists is the time we spend in contemplation. I realize how fraught my life outside was with the burden of living and learning how to behave among strangers. Even as we all spend most of our days laboring for the well-being of our community, we have time to pray and consider the mysteries.

I look back on what we were taught in catechism and later in the seminary and see it all very differently. It's easy for an outsider to imagine that we live in an unreal world, hidden away from the clamor and chaos of open society, but that's not true. We're a community of men, all different, all imperfect. The small scale of our community is like an amplifier. We're like atoms in a nuclear collider. But we also enjoy the grace of a contemplative life nourished by silence and beauty. Our community includes older, wiser men to whom we can turn for council. Life is full and by no means dull, as so many imagine. The life I lead now is scaled to who I am.

Whereas you, you are very much among the faithful. I hope you're enjoying your vocation as much as I am. You're doing the Lord's work among His people, dispensing the sacraments, counselling those who have lost their way, and dispensing mercy and compassion to those whom life has reefed. I often imagine you in your parish.

Do you find time for contemplation and prayer in your busy day?

Do you have friends and a wise father-confessor to turn to?

How are your Ma, Rosaire, and Lucienne? Lucienne must be in college now.

I love you, but not as your silence tells me you feared.

Fraternitas in nomine Patris, et Filii, et Spiritus Sancti.

Paolo

I turn again to the wine, not the cloying sweet wine of communion, but the dry, musky pinot that compresses my joys and fears into a manageable landscape. Sitting in my one livingroom chair amidst a swirl of heat-borne dust, I reread Paolo's letter, and my eyes fill with tears. I never told him of Rosaire's death, which I have yet to grieve myself, nor have I answered his first letter, as I promised I would.

I fold his letter carefully and re-insert it into the beautiful envelope and pour another glass of wine. I make a sandwich from a square, rubbery yellow cheese slice and a tomato I try to slice with a knife that's never been sharpened, rupturing the beautiful fruit. I gather the bits, fork them onto the cheese, and close the sandwich with a cover of billowy white bread, as I try to imagine the rich and heavy texture of Paolo's loaves.

My thoughts go back to my prison visit, and I wonder at the accumulated misery inside one building. I consider again the Church's teachings on the prerequisites of sin: understanding its sinful nature and willful commission. Of the sins I heard in prison, few seem to fit this definition: a child's effort to relieve his family poverty escalates into armed robberies, a Romeo and Juliet love affair becomes a rape, and a vengeful rage expressed to a parole board ensures a lifetime behind bars. God's silence and the vacuum of grace behind the bars and razor wire haunt me as I struggle to reconcile dogma with the pain and sadness I hear from those I meet. I wonder if Paolo, too, has doubts.

I recite another early morning Mass, heard only by my new altar boy, Eric Logan, who seems to enjoy enunciating his Latin responses. He's a clever kid and has pointed out to me the difference in pronunciation between ecclesiastical Latin and the academic Latin II he's taking in junior high school. After Mass as we're hanging up our vestments, he asks me if I know the Pope's phone number. Surprised at the question, I tell him I don't, and he answers with a broad smile, *"Et cum spiritu tuo,"* carefully enunciating the numbers 2-2-0. I laugh out loud, realizing I haven't heard myself laugh since my move to this parish. He tells me his Latin teacher told him the joke when he asked her about the difference between church Latin and school Latin.

After lunch, it's time to hear confessions again. I enter the confessional with my usual apprehension. I've been worried about Jimmy and his suicidal thoughts. I keep hoping he'll come back so I can talk with him outside the bounds of confession and find him help. But how could I ever help him feel loved, needed, or part of a family? How does one help one who has lost the will to live?

An older woman whose voice I've never heard begins her confession, explaining to me she's lived for sixteen years in a *Boston marriage.* I have no idea what she's talking about.

She lists a few venial sins and asks me the same question Ellen did.

"If I choose to live in a state of perpetual sin as a lesbian, can I ever truly be part of the communion of the faithful?

I know the answer is yes, and tell her so, qualifying it by adding, "but never in a state of grace."

"The Church doesn't forgive certain sins, does she?" she asks.

Again, confused, I try to answer. "The Church forgives sins for which a sinner is repentant, but the choice to live in a perpetual state of sin denies repentance and therefore absolution," I answer, recalling a seminary lecture on sin.

"So, loving someone's a sin?" she asks.

I answer that loving someone is not a sin, but homosexuality is an offense in the eyes of God.

"What makes you think our life together is sexual? What if we just prefer one another's company to the company of men? So, is our love still an offense against God?" she asks.

I'm in free fall. Sensing my mute confusion, she rises from the kneeler, saying, "Perhaps next time, you'll have an answer for me, or maybe you won't." I hear her leave the confessional.

I hear a dozen more confessions. I listen to the sins, offer absolution, and prescribe penance. I haven't sinned enough in my own life to be a good priest or to even understand and counsel those who have.

Dear Paolo,

I'm sorry for not answering your earlier letters. Reading them brings me such joy. It's as if I'm actually hearing your voice back in the chapel at St. John's. I reread them when I'm at a low point and know that, despite my thoughtless behavior when we parted, I still have a dear friend.

I'm overwhelmed by my priestly duties and realizing that I've no idea what I'm doing. As one charged with helping others through the spiritual ups and downs of their lives, I realize I've never had much of a life. My own has been one long evasion.

Just as I misunderstood and so betrayed our friendship when we parted, I feel I'm doing the same here every day. I fear the confessional. I hear things I don't understand and am asked for counsel I don't have. Do you ever feel at a loss? It sounds from your letter that your life is rich and full of grace and community. I long to try a slice of your bread.

I know you go to confession, but do you hear confessions? So many of the sins I hear in confession are alien to me. They're often an admission of an ongoing sinful-state, what we used to call "sins of perpetuity," like infidelities, divorce, suicidal thoughts, drunkenness, homosexuality. Does one grant absolution to such a sinner? I've denied absolution to several and left members of my parish in limbo as to whether they can ever receive God's grace through the sacraments. So much of what we learned in seminary makes no sense to me in real life. Are you having any of these thoughts?

I wish we could again be sitting quietly together in the chapel having this conversation instead of in the epistolary style of St. Paul.

I hope to come visit you someday at the Abbey. It sounds like the kind of life I had so hoped for. Your quiet, contemplative life is so different from my own confused life. I wish I could join you, but I've already broken my commitment to celibacy, although I hardly know how I did so or with whom. I was drunk.

Please don't give up on me. I cling to our friendship, even as I feel the Church is failing me and I, it.

In brotherly love,

Pierre

Bathed in the Blood

Later in the morning, the phone rings, a woman whose voice I don't recognize asks if I've seen Jimmy. I only know one Jimmy and, ignoring the bounds of confession, I answer, "No."

"You know him?" she asks. "I know he goes to confession sometimes at your church. Roger and I aren't Catholic, but Jimmy was raised Catholic before he came to live with us. Have you talked to him recently? He went fishing early this morning. It's one of the few things that seems to bring him any pleasure. I thought nothing of it until I saw my husband's rifle was missing from the open gun case. Jimmy's never shown any interest in hunting.

"Roger's coming home from work and we're going to look for him, but I thought I'd call to see if you'd seen him anywhere. He wasn't in school either."

"I haven't," I answer, "but I'll come over. Where do you live?"

I get in the car and follow her directions to their house which is only a few miles away. I arrive just as her husband pulls up. He seems angry.

"Had no business taking my gun. Jimmy's got no experience hunting and last fall I offered to take him deer hunting but he said he wasn't sure he could kill an animal. Imagine that! So, what's he doing with my gun?"

I introduce myself, saying only that I'd met Jimmy once at church and found him a likeable kid. Jimmy's mother emerges from the house and the three of us begin walking through the field behind their home to the creek flowing a few hundred yards behind their house.

"A boy needs lessons before he goes hunting. I had to go hunting twice with my father before he'd even let me touch his gun. Don't know what Jimmy 'as thinkin', takin' my gun without askin'. He doesn't ask for much, but we give him pretty much whatever he asks for, try to be good foster parents. Don't know what he's thinkin'. Let's go. I think I know where he's fishin'."

I follow Roger down to the creek. Mrs. Halverson walks behind me. The ground is spongy underfoot as we follow Roger trampling clumps of waist-high ferns down to the river's edge.

"The current slows behind this fallen-down tree and he often fishes around here," Roger says without turning around.

At the river bank, Roger turns left and follows a path along the river's bend. Far ahead of us now, he stops suddenly and yells to his wife to stay back.

I rush forward and see Jimmy lying in the muddy silt. There's no blood. His torso's fallen into the water and I see a stream of blood seeping from a clean wound in his temple eddying away rapidly in the stream. A fishing rod with a small casting reel lies propped on a Y-shaped whittled branch nearby, its line taut in the slow current. A Mossberg 30.06 lies next to him in a few inches of water nearby. The bluing on its shiny barrel glistens in the bright sun.

Roger grabs the gun and shakes the water off, wipes the barrel on his handkerchief and lays it in the dry ferns. Mrs. Halverson catches up with us, sees Jimmy in the water, lets out a loud wail, and covers her face as she turns away.

Aghast, I stare at Jimmy's unfamiliar face looking up from the shallow water, as the monotone of his confession replays itself in my head.

"I just don't want to be alive any more. I don't have any friends. I'm not good at anything like sports or studies. Kids pay no attention to me. They don't even care enough to tease me. It's like I'm not there."

I wade into the water in my cassock and lift Jimmy from the water and silt, holding him to my chest as I walk backwards up onto dry land.

My mind's racing with my familiar *man-of-God* directives. What comes first? Do I console the distraught Mrs. Halverson? calm the confused and angry Mr. Halverson? administer last rites to Jimmy? call the police and answer their questions?

I drag Jimmy up into the dry ferns and lay him down. A sharp constriction in my chest leaves me short of breath, lunging for air. Trying to catch my breath, I hear myself sobbing. My wet cassock clings to me like a shroud.

Overtaken by an unfamiliar sadness and tears, I suddenly realize I can't help anyone here. I try in vain to gather myself. When my own father and brother died, I felt only a mute and lingering fear. But somehow in his death, a stranger has managed to share the sadness he feels and confessed to me. The shame I feel at not knowing how to help him when he sought my help is lost in my own uncontrollable sadness.

I sit down next to Jimmy. Cradling his head as I try to catch my breath, I keep repeating, "I'm sorry. I'm so sorry."

I'm apologizing to a stranger I only met once in the shadows of the confessional and only now in the sunlight can I see the sad light in his young face.

Mr. Halverson leaves to call the police, taking his gun with him and leaving Mrs. Halverson on the bank with me and Jimmy. Mrs. Halverson weeps quietly, standing next to us, her head turned away.

I hear two squad cars and an ambulance brake to a halt on the street beside the Halverson's. Mr. Halverson leads three officers and two stretcher-bearers to where the three of us are on the bank.

I don't remember returning home or falling asleep that night. I remember only Jimmy's face, the pale light of his loneliness in the shallow water and knowing I'd absorbed and was feeling all the sadness he left behind.

A Whiff of Scandal

The following week, I get a call from a Mrs. Halverson asking if she might come by the rectory and speak with me. We agree on a time, she comes, and I invite her in.

"How are you doing?" I ask her. "How can I help you?" She settles uncomfortably into my couch and self-consciously crosses her legs. She looks down and I sense she's going to cry. I ask if she'd like a glass of water and, sniffling, she shakes her head sideways. I realize I'm staring at the landscape of blue varicose veins on her calves and turn away.

"I still can't believe it. I knew he was sad, kept mostly to himself, but he seemed to get some pleasure from the airplane models he built and occasionally flew in the meadow behind our house and fishing for bass in the creek. Then, suddenly, he's gone. Even though we fostered him, it was like he was my own kin. Not sure Roger ever quite felt that way, but he treated Jimmy good and taught him things he needed to know to get on in life.

"How is Roger?" I ask.

"At first, he was angry Jimmy'd taken his rifle without asking. Roger's first reactions sometimes can be selfish but he's a good man and always comes around.

"We still can't make any sense of it. Jimmy didn't talk much but didn't seem like he was that unhappy. When he wasn't at school or working at the D.Q., he mostly read western stories, built his models, or fished out behind the house."

"What can I do?" I ask as the unfamiliar sadness wells up in me again and I fear losing the composure I'll need to help Mrs. Halverson.

"Did he ever talk to you about his feelings? Did you have any worries about him? Does this mean he can't be buried in the Church and have a funeral Mass?" she continues.

Mrs. Halverson begins to sob. I reach over and take her forearm with one hand and put the other on her shoulder, surprised to feel her collarbone beneath the frail shoulder.

"I'm so sorry. I didn't know Jimmy well, other than to see him occasionally at Sunday Mass. Was he a shy boy? Did he have friends at school? How did they take the news of his death?"

"Jimmy had no friends we knew of. Did he ever talk with you, Father? Did he go to confession? He often rode off on his bike, telling us he'd be back, that he was going to confession."

"I hear so many confessions. I can't remember them all and have no specific memory of Jimmy in confession," I lie, "and, if I did, I'm bound by the sacrament of confession to keep whatever he might have said between him and God.

"What do you and Mr. Halverson want to happen?" I ask.

"Well, you know, he wasn't our natural son. We fostered him when he was about seven. He came from a family where the father was in jail and the mother was incapacitated and couldn't care for him. That's all we know. He was such a sweet boy, very quiet, but so sweet. We'd like him to have a funeral Mass and be buried in the Church cemetery."

"Suicide's an offense against God, a mortal sin. But what little of Jimmy I knew, I felt he was a good boy and never hurt anyone. That counts for something in my world.

"Let me see what I can do. I will call you and Mr. Halverson. I need a day to think about it. You'll hear from me tomorrow. I'm so sorry. Go in peace."

I help her up off the couch and, hold her hand as she walks sobbing quietly. I lead her to the door.

I call the following day. Mr. Halverson answers and I express my condolences at Jimmy's death, saying that I remember him from church and occasional visits to confession. Mr. Halverson tells me that the police have investigated their foster son's death and have called it a suicide.

"Meg and I are embarrassed, wondering if people will think we didn't do a good job bringing him up, but everyone always told us what a nice boy he was and that even as a young man, he was polite, only that he kept largely to himself. Seems like his life wasn't that bad. Meg and I did the best we could and saw to it that he got what he needed. He just didn't seem that motivated, although he worked regular and all. Makes no sense to us."

"I understand," I answer. "My memory of Jimmy is that he was a good boy. I think his sadness just overwhelmed his will to live."

"But suicide is a crime and a mortal sin. What about that?" Mr. Halverson continues.

"There's nothing for you or the police to do. No charge will be brought. No one will judge you and Meg for your kindness in raising Jimmy. I will say a solemn high mass here at Holy Family for the salvation of his soul and he'll be buried at Ste. Anne's in consecrated ground. You needn't worry."

"But won't you get in trouble? Suicides aren't supposed to be buried alongside regular folks."

"Jimmy was regular folk. He simply found little joy in his life.

He's not alone and will be forgiven by his God. Leave the rest to me."

With that, I again offer my condolences and ask Mr. and Mrs. Halverson to come by the church tomorrow to make arrangements for Jimmy's mass and burial.

The first call I get the next day is from the Westover Funeral Home. A solemn-voiced Mr. DiLucca says he is calling about arrangements for Jimmy Halverson's funeral. He understands from the family that there will be a funeral mass, followed by burial in the church cemetery. He further intones that he "expects that, in their grief, they misunderstood their discussion with me since the nature of their son's death precludes a Christian burial."

I answer that his business is to embalm and deliver to the Halversons their son's remains in a casket of their choice and that I will handle the religious details. There is a long silence, followed by "As you wish, Father Pierre," and then a dial tone. This will not be my last call on the subject.

I sit down at the kitchen table and nurse a mug of cold coffee, trying to make sense of what I've done.

As is so often the case, the flame of scandal is ignited by one parishioner who'd heard that "a suicide" was to be treated like a regular churchgoer "in a state of grace" and would be mourned and interred as such. The arsonous gossip spreads quickly, bringing more shame and sadness on the bereft Halversons.

At the funeral mass, I notice that some regulars are missing from the service. The Westover community is so small that many townsfolk come to all funerals to express condolences, as most of the families know one another directly or informally. My decision to treat Jimmy as if he died in a state of grace divides my parish into those who believe I acted compassionately to Jimmy and his foster family, and other more righteous parishioners who quietly share their feelings that burying Jimmy alongside their own kin diminishes their own righteousness.

Mr. DiLucca telephones the bishop, who calls me, asking for an explanation.

I explain that I knew Jimmy only in confession and suggest to the bishop that Church doctrine on self-harm doesn't consider life circumstances or psychological ones. As his father-confessor, I felt it was within my authority to grant him absolution after his death by his own hand. I tell the bishop of Jimmy's kindness and sense of responsibility to his foster parents and say I simply couldn't ignore or judge the paralyzing sadness that so distorted Jimmy's view of life. I remind him that a prerequisite of sin is willful knowledge, not despair.

My rationale falls on deaf ears, and the question of my judgment is eclipsed by increasing pressure on the Church to spread what little clergy they have among dwindling parishes. So the bishop reassigns errant priests to parishes well beyond the shadow of the scandal they've created.

A Breakdown

It's again time for me to make my monthly report and confession to Father Conran. I leave the rectory in early afternoon and begin the drive to Bennington. Driving south, I notice for the first time the loose paper sticker dangling behind my rearview mirror. A scrawl on it indicates my rusting Rambler American should have been inspected on or before the eighth month of this year — yet another sign of how heedless I've been about life's exigencies. I promise myself I'll get my car inspected the following week. I'll ask one of my parishioners on Sunday what garage they'd recommend in Westover.

As I cross the Green Mountains, a heavy fog settles in, and I turn on my low beams. It's 2:30 and feels like dusk. The acrid smell of exhaust inside the car forces me to open a window and then I hear the screech of metal on metal. I've no idea where it's coming from. The air inside the car clears, but the cold forces me to close the window. Suddenly, the car begins to shudder and finally comes to a stop as I shift into neutral and coast onto the unpaved shoulder.

I'm about three miles from Bennington. I get out into the fog and see smoke billowing out of the radiator grill. I know there's no point in trying to restart the car. I can't figure out how to open the hood and just stand there staring at it. If I could open it, I've no idea what to look for. Rosaire would be under the hood and have diagnosed, if not fixed, the problem. After some twenty minutes of my looking and feeling foolish, a sheriff pulls up behind me and turns on his light. Seeing my collar, he dispenses with the formalities of license and registration. He seems a good sort and greets me as "Father."

"Looks like your Rambler may need last rites, Father. I'd guess from the smoke and smell the engine seized up and, given the body rot around your fenders and running boards, I doubt she's worth rebuilding." I suddenly wonder why he assumes my car's female.

"I expect you're right, officer. Can I get a ride into town? I'm going into see my colleague, Father Conran at St Mary's. I'll get someone from Bennington to haul it away."

"Probably worth $100 minimum in parts and scrap metal, so don't let these shysters charge you anything. Just tell them they can have car in exchange for hauling it away."

"Thanks for the advice. I don't know much about cars but I'll have to learn someday if I'm going to keep driving them, I expect."

"Hop in and I'll give you a ride to the church. I'm sure Father Conran will offer you a toddy to drown your sorrows."

I welcome the cruiser's warm interior and lack of exhaust smell… just the pine incense cutout dangling from the rearview mirror.

"Good luck, shouldn't be too hard getting a bus home. Tho' I bet Father Conran has a sinner among his flock'd give you a ride home in exchange for forgiveness. Ask him. Tell 'em his old altar boy, Billy Goddard, promised he'd get'cha home. He'll remember me… if not from the altar, from the confessional… and get your next car inspected," he adds with a laugh. With that, the sheriff drives away.

I push the doorbell button by the rectory entrance and hear Father Conran's heavy footsteps coming down the hall.

"Greetings, my lad, your failures have been announced. Come in, long walk?"

I greet Father Conran sheepishly and express my gratitude to his parishioner for my rescue.

"Oh, Billy's a good sort. Hit that existential tipping point as a young man, as so many young men do. Do I stay a bad boy or become a good man? Each has its benefits and its seductions. Besides, there's always confession, penance, and redemption if one changes his mind. How ya been, Padre?"

"I've been fine, Father, and you?"

"Don't call me 'Father.' We're colleagues. My name is *Michael Conran.* Family calls me 'Mick.' Probably better for you to call me 'Mike,' like most others do, even though I am a Mick. We don't use terms like that anymore. But we're bound by the confidentiality of confession...right? That's why you're here, right?... to tell me you've abused yourself again?"

"And to make my parish report," I answer, embarrassed and over-whelmed by Father Conran's burst of inquiry.

"Well, first things first... let's get you back in a state of grace so we can have a nip and some supper before I get Alton to run you back to Westover."

Father Conran slips on his stole, and I follow him over to the church, where he'll hear my confession.

"When we get to be friends and you trust me more than you do now, I can hear your confession over a nice brandy, instead of in a stuffy confessional closet reeking of sin. But it's too early for that. Right now, I expect you feel safer in the familiar shadows with a grill between us. I'll bet you don't have any sins beyond the one we both know and like. But I get ahead of myself. Wait until we get inside and do it right, like how you're used to."

Once inside the confessional, Father Conran listens to my opening confessional prayers and my pathetic litany of sins, then says "God and

I have forgiven you for your sexual transgression; have you forgiven yourself? Did you learn anything from it?"

I'm again at a loss for words and say only that I'm still trying to remember and understand what happened. Thankfully, he lets the matter rest and moves on to my penance and absolution.

"Now, I must go and celebrate the five o'clock Mass for those filling up my pews outside. After Mass, let's celebrate your newfound state of grace with a drink and some supper. I want to hear your parish report, such as it is. I've heard your automotive report; I understand the bishop is reassigning you for your transgressions; tell me more when I return."

With that dismissal, I hear Father Conran leave the confessional for the sacristy. I rise and leave in his wake, taking a seat in a nearby empty pew.

Father Conran's homily is on Mary Magdalene and the historical ambiguity of her reputation in the Church. In the western Catholic and later Protestant traditions, she was the repentant prostitute who followed Jesus and washed his feet with her hair. Forgiven by Christ, she's with Mary at his resurrection after the crucifixion.

Father Conran goes on to explain that the London asylum for insane women, *Magdalene* or *Maudlin* Hospital, was named for her, as were the *Magdalene Laundries* in Ireland where wayward girls were consigned to years of hand-washing the clothes and bedlinen of others with lye soap to atone for their sins of the flesh, just as Mary washed Christ's feet with her hair. He adds that our Church meted out these fierce penances to "fallen young woman," while never acknowledging that men usually initiate and account for their sins of the flesh — often family members, priests, and the men whose linen they must wash.

In the Eastern Rites, he explains, Mary Magdalene is portrayed as a virgin during her time with Christ; he notes there are no allusions in the four gospels to her as a "fallen woman" until Pope Gregory the First delivers a sermon in the sixth century in which he describes her as a harlot.

Father Conran quotes Pope Gregory's sermon on the subject.

She whom Luke calls the sinful woman, whom John calls Mary, we believe to be the Mary from whom seven devils were ejected according to Mark. What did these seven devils signify, if not all the vices? It is clear that the woman previously used the unguent to perfume her flesh in forbidden acts. What she therefore displayed more scandalously, she was now offering to God in a more praiseworthy manner. She had coveted with earthly eyes, but now through penitence these are consumed with tears. She displayed her hair to set off her face, but now her hair dries her tears. She had spoken proud things with her mouth, but in kissing the Lord's feet, she now planted her mouth on the Redeemer's feet. For every delight, therefore, she had had in herself, she now immolated herself. She turned the mass of her crimes to virtues, in order to serve God entirely in penance. (Pope Gregory the Great homily XXXIII)

With a wink and flourish, Father Conran implies that Pope Gregory is enjoying his erotic portrayal of Mary of Magdala. He concludes his sermon on the ambiguity of Mary Magdalene's reputation by counselling his parishioners not to judge others and to remember that history has always consigned responsibility for sins of the flesh to women and that their judges are always men.

I've no idea what to make of this sermon and can't imagine writing or delivering a sermon that so challenges the Church's doctrine.

After receiving communion and the final blessing, I walk over to the rectory to wait for Father Conran in his library.

Exhausted, I fall asleep sitting in an oversized mission-style chair in Father Conran's library. I wake up feeling someone wrapping my fingers around a warm brandy snifter.

"I'm sorry, Father, I think the day's excitement has taken its toll," I say in an embarrassed whisper.

"My name's Mike, and if you ever want absolution again, you'd better call me by name, not my title. I'm not going to call you Father Pierre, so get used to it... Pierre and Mike," he snaps, taking a sip from his own glass. But it's hard to overcome an upbringing in which deference to age, uniform, wealth, and clergy are givens.

"Okay then, Mike. I'll try," I offer with considerable discomfort.

"Good, then here's to your first sexual experience," he says raising his glass.

"I only wish I could remember more of it," I answer, not daring to admit I wish it'd never happened.

"One learns much from what one hears in the confessional, but only personal experience imparts wisdom. A good father-confessor needs to have committed sins to fully appreciate them. Besides, true guilt or innocence can hardly be determined from an index of doctrinal transgressions.

"Most sins, like acts of compassion, are better understood in life's *accidents* — *accidents* in the Latin sense, meaning *contextually*. That's why we talk about "discernment." They probably didn't teach you that in seminary. It can't be taught. Life's hardships and our own transgressions enrich us deeply and can only be understood through contemplation, not facile judgments of good or evil.

"Is a Catholic woman who leaves her abusive husband for fear of being injured or killed in a state of mortal sin? Don't answer, just think.

"The Catholic woman who secretly aborts her fifth pregnancy because contraception is denied to her by the Church and her husband won't wear a condom…she has neither enough resources or energy left to raise yet another child and can't rely on her husband or family to raise the child…is she truly a murderer as the Church likes to say? Don't answer, just think.

"Is the young man born with a sexual preference for men, who brings the same level of morality and respect to his relationship with another man as he would to a woman, deserving of consignment to hell? Do we not already consign him to hell on earth with a canon that rejects him, denies him the sacraments or a place in a community of love and grace?

Many sins were, in fact, made up by men to serve their own purposes.

"In the Second Lateran Council in the twelfth century, priestly celibacy was adopted mostly to further enrich the Church. Too many priests were leaving their land and worldly goods to their sons and daughters instead of the Church, so the Church hierarchy eliminated marriage and childbearing — at least in wedlock — as an option for priests.

"There are no simple answers, although our Church would have us believe there are.

"Are the seven deadly sins in fact mortal sins, or merely aspects of human behavior? Today, we understand there are psychological and physical dependencies: gluttony, fornication, and avarice; the others: pride, despondency, wrath, and sloth are traits of the psyche that may lead us into sin but are not *per se* sinful until one acts on them.

"We can never understand true evil in the abstract, outside of its occurrence. Some even try to make the case that evil doesn't exist. Is the pedophile, preyed upon as a child by a trusted adult, a sinner or a student? Our job is to counter evil where we find it, counsel, forgive, and withhold personal judgment.

"Is the priest, in a moment of loneliness and lust who succumbs to a seduction and feels badly about it, any more or less a priest?

"At your young age, you have almost two-thirds of your life ahead of you before you attain your biblical three score and ten. There's time enough ahead to understand that you'll never know all the answers. Wisdom is knowledge of our own ignorance in the face of the divine.

"Before you come next month, read *The Legend of the Grand Inquisitor*. It's a parable within Dostoevsky's *The Brothers Karamazov*. One brother, Dmitri, a sybarite, tells his brother, Alexei, a monk, a story in which Christ comes back to earth during the Inquisition and is arrested by the Inquisitor, even as he knows he is arresting the Son of God. Your penance will be to explain the parable to me next month.

"Now then... that's enough of a speech! I hear through the grapevine that the bishop's pissed at you for blessing a young boy who killed himself and burying him next to the self-righteous. What say you, lad?"

"I know the Church's teaching on suicides," I say. "I know it's a mortal sin and that suicides are condemned to even more hell than they experience on earth, but it made no sense to me then and doesn't now.

"I was there after his death and pulled him from the riverbank. I never felt such sadness in my life. It was as if my own son died and I did nothing to prevent it. Besides, I felt complicit. He'd confessed his thoughts of suicide to me and I did nothing. I tried to find him afterward to talk with him, but I didn't try hard enough."

"You tried; that's more than most do. What would you do differently today? Would you break the bonds of confession and try to find and help him? You did all you could do. You forgave him his sin and offered him a Mass of Christian Burial and a resting place among God's other sinners. You felt his sadness. You are no different. Blessing on you. Don't worry about the bishop. He's an ass, always has been. Remember, Christ rode on an ass.

"Let's eat. My stew is always bubbling on the stove, and Millie brought me another loaf of Irish soda bread."

After supper, there's a knock on the rectory door, and a decrepit man comes into the kitchen.

"Meet Alton, your chauffer. He'll drive you back to Westover in style. Alton is also my chauffeur when I overindulge in the earthly spirits. Alton, meet Pierre."

Riding home in a rusty pickup truck, I fall asleep again, despite the roar of a missing muffler and tailpipe, and sleep soundly until Alton wakes me up with a pat on the shoulder. I wake up feeling guilty for having fallen asleep and ignored my driver. I thank him, asking if he'd like to come in for a coffee. He flashes me a tattered card laminated in plastic that says, "Hi, I'm Alton. I'm deaf and dumb. I understand sign language and written words. If you must talk to me, write me a note."

I thank him and put my hand on his shoulder. He smiles. I leave the truck, and Alton drives off without ever turning off the ignition.

As I'm falling asleep trying to make sense of my conversation with Father Conran, it occurs to me that Alton can't hear the roar of his truck.

A New Assignment

I've been at this job now for some seven years. It feels more like a poorly paid job than a spiritual avocation. I have a joyless house with sagging upholstery, cigarette burns and greasy surfaces everywhere, a waning number of elderly parishioners in my church, a Congolese priest who covers for me when I'm sick or visiting home and, with Ma's help, a used VW Beetle to replace my Rambler.

The following month I'm reassigned to a parish in Graniteville, Vermont, landing me much closer to Ma and Jeanine.

The inauspicious nature of my new location's name is not lost on me, as my new parish includes the quarries my father worked in and the finishing sheds filled with the granite dust glittering in the afternoon sunlight that slowly killed so many quarrymen. My new parish covers East Barre, Websterville, and Graniteville; the collective population is about 3000. Many of the quarry workers are of Italian descent; most in the tri-town area are practicing Catholics, predominantly Italian, but Irish and French Canadian as well.

Lucienne is now teaching history and geography at Corpus Christi High School in Burlington. Ma retired last year when the Phillips family and a skeleton crew of domestics decamped for Rhode Island's shores. Ma was given a sendoff commensurate with the Phillips's generosity and affection for her. I could not attend, but Lucienne and Jeanine were there. Ma was also given a modest pension in deference to her long service, although she was surprised to learn that she was expected to return the threadbare service uniforms she had worn for thirty-two years.

When it comes time to move to Graniteville, a few of my Westover parishioners stop by to wish me well or pause on the church steps after Sunday Mass to say good-bye. Others seem hardly to notice my departure. The move is easy, as my few possessions fit comfortably in my VW.

The faith Paolo and I studied together now seems so remote from what I encounter as a parish priest, the catechism so irrelevant, I sometimes find myself questioning the very existence of sin.

I hear the anger, sadness, pain, abuse, fear, drudgery, and loneliness of those who frequent my confessional. My own joyless existence further distances me from what I learned in seminary. In confession, I sometimes feel like a child sitting in the vast Odeon movie theater we went to in Barre when we were kids, except, sitting in total darkness after the projector bulb fails, I hear only the soundtrack for a grownup movie beyond my comprehension. I wish Paolo wasn't so far away.

I keep a small collection of dirty magazines hidden under my mattress. They've begun appearing in some variety stores and gas stations. I buy one only when I'm out of town and in civilian clothes. I'm ashamed of them, much less using them, but I can no more do without them than my cocktails.

From their tawdry images, I've reconstructed in my imagination what happened between me and Ellen that night, wondering how much of my role was instinctual and what she must have taught me. I wonder if she's happy in her new relationship.

The occasional thought of looking for her only underscores the pathos of my existence. Would she even remember me? Is she happy with her lover? So much time has passed. How much longer will I adolesce before I'm an adult?

Ma in Decline

The steep decline in men and women entering religious vocations has put further pressure on the diocese as it tries in vain to supply parishes with priests and teaching nuns. Circuit riders are pressed into service in some rural areas and other sparse parishes simply close, desanctify and sell their churches. The tradition in Irish, French, Polish, and Italian families of giving one child to the Lord has become a relic of the past. Under this stress, the Vermont bishop ignores renegade priests unless he gets serious complaints. Luckily, my parishioners mostly seem to like and welcome me.

Since my move to Graniteville, Jeanine's been calling me with worrying reports of Ma's memory lapses. I call Lucienne to ask what she knows, and she says that she and Jeanine have been in regular touch and that Ma can no longer be left alone. Burned pots, doors left open, sinks left running, hygiene lapses, and repetitive questions make clear that Ma's becoming a danger to herself.

Two months later, Jeanine is diagnosed with lung cancer. We're all caught off guard. Her cancer progresses rapidly, metastasizing in the spring. She dies in the hospital surrounded by her daughter Libby, Lucienne, Ma, and me. Ma seems not to understand why we're gathered around Jeanine's hospital bed. It's clear to Lucienne and me that one of us must take over her care with Jeanine gone.

Lucienne is sharing an apartment in Burlington with two aged nuns in a disused convent and has no room for Ma. I volunteer to take

Ma, as the rectory I now live is the product of an earlier and more prosperous era in the Church's history and there are three bedrooms in addition to mine. Following Father Conran's example, I keep them open as short-term shelter for the occasional down-on-their-luck parishioner — a recovering alcoholic, rejected spouse, or runaway teen. I'm aware that rumors will take root should I offer a room to a female, but I've become inured to gossip. I currently have a relapsed alcoholic named Cecil in the back room, who has, so far, kept his promise not to drink.

When I first ask Ma to come live with me, she just seems confused — another scared person needing refuge. I know that the personal chaos that landed Cecil at my door will resolve if he remains sober and apart from whatever derailed him earlier. The calm boredom of rectory life offers a void within which one may regain a sense of self. My few boarders are usually content just to be left alone to lick their wounds, have meals, privacy, and a warm bed. I don't realize that Ma will never get well or find herself but will only decline further and require more care.

Ma settles in to her new room and seems content for the first few days, but the unfamiliar surroundings into which she awakes each morning scare her, and she asks me where she is and why she lives in this big house. She asks repeatedly where Jeanine, Lucienne, and Rosaire are, and I explain each day that Rosaire died in the war and Jeanine died of cancer, and that Lucienne is fine and is teaching school in Burlington. But the maelstrom of fear, confusion, and anger inside Ma's head is unrelieved by my explanations and only seeds the storm clouds of her fear and confusion. Ma nods, but her face shows little sign of comprehension. I know this conversation will repeat itself several times during the day.

To ensure her safety and hygiene, I'm reduced to bathing her every few days, and her girlhood modesty turns to shame when I help her undress and sit down in the tub. She sees me as a deviant rather than the nurse I've become. My own feelings are confused and conflicted. I never thought to see my mother unclothed and the image of her nakedness conflicts with the idealized female images I see in my dirty magazines.

It's getting harder to fulfill my clerical duties and continue to care for Ma. Even as I understand that caring for her in her decline is at the heart of my faith, I can no longer do both. Ma requires more and more surveillance.

I invite a woman named Clarisse Rochefolle, who lost her home when her husband decamped for Canada taking their son, to move into the room down the hall from Ma. Clarissse sees my fatigue and confusion and offers to care for Ma fulltime if I can arrange for a modest stipend and let her remain in the rectory for a time. Exhausted, I agree without a second thought. Having assumed legal and financial responsibility for Ma, I give Clarisse Ma's pension income in exchange for her care, for which she is grateful. Ma seems more comfortable with this stranger of her own sex than with her son.

Cecil, Clarisse, and I take turns preparing evening meals, and I use the quiet time after our communal supper to write Paolo. We've maintained our correspondence over the years as if our friendship was never cut short by my hasty judgment. In the ensuing years, I've heard the confessions of and met homosexual men and women and see them now as I see Paolo. I also know that my judgment was both a learned and defensive response, deeply at odds with my study of the life of Christ, on which I rely more now as a moral text than Church doctrine.

I'm no longer shocked by what I hear in confession, nor do I judge those whose sins I hear, regardless of their circumstances. I ignore the Church's Jesuitical digressions on sin, absolution, and penance that I so readily accepted in catechism and seminary. I know my detours from doctrine will get me in trouble again, but my life is increasingly full, and I've come to care less about consequences and more about compassion as I try to understand and forgive the human frailty I find in myself and others. I think often of Jimmy and wish that I could have known him as he grew into a man.

Transubstantiation

Dear Paolo,

Life continues here in Vermont. I envy you your cloistered community and sometimes imagine myself having time to study, think, pray, and work with my hands in silence and natural light, rather than addressing the candlelit transactions of parish priesthood: confessions, funerals, confirmations, weddings, baptisms, clerical accounting, and writing sermons. My confreres subscribe to a "homily service" that mails them a written sermon conforming to the ecclesiastical calendar. They can personalize or just read it . . . seems so far removed from the idea of talking with one's parishioners, although I find it tempting with all there is to do.

As I get older, the faith we shared is waning in me. Its loss has made room in my soul for a deeper connection to the people I serve. I so often think of our long talks together about the spiritual tension between the Roman curia with their Canon Law and the liberation theologists whose empathy for the poor, we both agreed, more closely emulated Christ's own compassion.

My dear friend and early mentor, Father Conran, died of a heart attack last week in his sleep. After my diocesan reassignment, we spoke occasionally by phone. He always called me on my birthday and I never called him, for which I still feel guilt. I always wished that I had lived life as he had. He often said he'd "committed all the sins necessary to become a good priest and recommitted them just often enough to meet his sheep in their pasture instead of in his paddock." He hated hypocrisy and the holier-than-thou attitude of so many of our peers. He distained false piety and claimed it was one of the few truly mortal sins. I miss him as I miss you.

Last month, he gave me an assignment which I've not completed. I was to read "The Legend of the Grand Inquisitor" and explain it to him on my next visit. His death intervened, and I promised myself I would complete the assignment. Have you ever read it? Perhaps, one day we could discuss it.

Ma is living with me and declining rapidly. She suffers from senile dementia and no longer knows me. When I greet her, she just looks at me quizzically as if I am somehow familiar to her, but she can't make the connection that I'm her son. A lovely woman lives in the rectory and cares for her. I am so grateful, as I couldn't do both. Ma requires fulltime oversight, and Clarisse seems to love caring for her. The only time Ma ever smiles is in her company. I know Ma has no desire to go on living as she is. Her doctor tells me her heart is strong, though, and she could live another decade. I can't imagine such an existence. She lives in constant confusion and fear except when Clarisse is with her.

I had a young parishioner many years ago who killed himself. In his one confession, I heard his wish to finally end the sadness, sorrow, and isolation that haunted him. I wonder if Ma feels that way.

I hope you are well and that your loaves are multiplying. I do hope our paths meet again. Kentucky seems so far from Graniteville.

In brotherly love,

Pierre

P.S. Can you mail me a loaf of your bread?

Dirty Thoughts and Deeds

When I first became a parish priest, sitting in the confessional waiting for the sound of the curtain on either side to be withdrawn, I was always anxious. I'd hear a parishioner kneel and wait for me to open the slide. I'd pause to gather my wits, as I heard to them shifting their weight on the uncomfortable kneeler. But now, the dark quiet of the confessional is a source of peace. I look forward to my talks with those who come to me for the absolution of a God in whom I no longer believe. They don't need my forgiveness, as I don't judge them. They come for my guidance and God's absolution … easy enough for me to give.

Often as I wait for someone to come in, Louis Brusa's magnificent gravestone for his parents, The Bored Angel, appears to me, just as it was when Pa took me and Rosaire there when we were little.

I open the slide and hear a familiar voice — one of our older church members — and I know what's coming.

"Bless me, Father, for I have sinned, and it's been three weeks since my last confession. As you'll remember, I am a widower. My Kathy died nine years back, and I still miss her every day. I accuse myself of masturbating twice since my last confession. I don't look at dirty pictures like so many do nowadays. I don't like seeing 'em smutty calendars where I get my car fixed neither. 'Stead, I think of my Kathy and how much pleasure and joy we brought each other. She was my light and I miss her to this day. I know it's a mortal sin and I ask your absolution, Father, and God's forgiveness."

I've heard this confession before and always used to give my rote response, "Pray to the Virgin and ask for purity of thought," a repetition of the empty advice I was given as a child. I no longer confess my own occasional masturbation.

This time I say, "You're making love to the memory of someone you loved very much and that is hardly a sin. There's no need to ask either God or me to forgive you. Your only penance is to forgive yourself, since you still believe it's a sin. You honor your Kathy's memory. Go in peace."

I close the slide not waiting for a protest. The penitent remains for some time and finally rises and leaves. I hear two more confessions in which I also struggle to find sin and return to the rectory for a late afternoon sip of my scotch and tea.

I still think of Ellen and wonder how she is. My jumbled memory of that night reminds me uncomfortably of the magazines under my mattress. The first time I had the courage to buy such a magazine, it had four or five vivacious women who looked like they were enjoying their work. These "calendar girls" looked at once approachable and feisty — not to be crossed. They were the same women painted on the engine cowls of fighter planes in the war and or on oil-stained calendars in car repair shops over the tool bench. I wonder what would happen if these earlier glossy companions of us lonely priests, soldiers, truckers, and mechanics ever actually came into our lives. Most of us, I believe, would be at a loss as to what to do or say. We really only intend these displays to convey to other men and women our sexual prowess, not our deep insecurities.

Over the years if I'm out of town, I add a magazine here and there to my small collection when I stop at a convenience store for a coffee or sandwich. As the array of magazines on the racks grows,

I notice a distinct change in the demeanor of the women inside. The come-hither smiles of the earlier "calendar girls," challenge one to earn their attention and affection before any dalliance might ever be possible. But the looks of the women whose body parts I stare at now seem more like defenseless girls than powerful sirens, as their eyes elude the pornographer.

As a child, I was taught that looking at images of naked women was a sin. I've long known that my use of pornography is lonely and exploitive, distancing me from the tenderness and affection I crave. I can no longer look into the eyes of its subjects. Did I use these magazines to sustain my celibacy?

When I look at these young women's faces, my sadness overwhelms any sexual response. I put my seven magazines into a used manila envelope and remove the address and the return address. I slide it under my VW seat to discard next time I'm at a gas station.

I've come to understand that pornography distracts us from something more stimulating...the naturally occurring eroticism that arouses but demeans no one and ensures our survival as a species. Unlike the blunt instrument of pornography, eroticism is a grace, catching us unaware, never clinical, just a resonance...perhaps in an unfamiliar smile, the gentle rise of breasts beneath a blouse at the intake of breath, the unsought glance into a sleeveless blouse or décolletage. It's neither posed nor affected and may even arise in nature... a moss-covered clearing, waterfall, or birdsong that recalls a former tryst. We're surprised and engaged by our arousal. Since disposing of my sad images, I've become much more aware of eroticism's power over me and fear it less.

The following Sunday I deliver a sermon on pornography. I have no idea how it will be perceived. I talk about how pervasive it's become and the number of confessions I hear from young boys who have access to it and use it.

I used to write out sermons in full, make several editing passes, and then read them to my parishioners at Mass, taking care to look up as often as possible without losing my place in the text. Now I'm more comfortable adlibbing from the pulpit. Not until I've delivered it the following Sunday does it occur to me that my comments might betray a familiarity with my chosen topic.

I don't frame my homily in the context of good or evil, or even sin, but rather how pornography reduces its models of both sexes to a distant and purely carnal relationship — all pretty normal homiletic fare. I recall from my own earlier years how intensely I imagined girls in my class and conclude that the natural erotic drive derives from what is unfamiliar or unknown, what may only be glimpsed in a figure or a smile. Only when I digress on how the familiarity of pornography's intimate anatomical imagery soon depletes the natural intrigue and power of Eros of its mystery, do I begin to see parishioners look at each other questioningly.

I know from experience that when I began buying and looking at pornography, the unknown soon became familiar, clinical; its erotic energy dissipated into trivial addiction. I wanted more for the young men and women I counselled.

I think of my conversation with Father Conran about masturbation, to which we both confessed back then. I asked if him he looked at dirty magazines and he answered, "No need... beautiful women just occur to me."

Windsor Prison

I've become a regular at the Windsor Prison. The prison was built during the presidency of Thomas Jefferson and doesn't appear much improved since that time. It's a barbaric affair, the oldest state prison in continuous operation in the United States. Each time I visit the few men who've asked for my counsel, I'm amazed at the harsh conditions of their confinement.

My favorite among them is Clem Mason. Clem's been there for forty-eight of his seventy-three years. In the sentencing phase of his trial, Clem was given a life sentence in lieu of hanging, after a Congregationalist minister begged judge and jury to spare his children the sight of his public execution. The same minister, the Reverend Philo Cosgrove, made a similar plea several decades later to the State Legislature and the death penalty in Vermont ended for good.

Clem's in good health mostly and has been scheduled for "compassionate release" because of his advanced age. His youthful crime was the impulsive murder of a farrier over his belief that the farrier had permanently and purposefully lamed his beloved logging horse, Milly, by using horseshoe nails he forged too long for Milly's hooves. Willy knocked the farrier dead with one of his driving hammers and then shoveled glowing coke from his forge onto his lifeless body. The crime was so vicious that a hue and cry went up for his hanging even before the trial convened in the Windsor Courthouse.

Clem never denied his crime. In fact, the following day he expressed his regret to the sheriff, saying only "a rage that burst into me" when he thought of the pain and suffering the farrier had caused his horse. Neither judge nor jury was sympathetic, and when the two-day trial ended, Clem was remanded to the prison next door to serve out the rest of his life in a five-by-eight-foot cell. At sentencing, he said his only regret was the loss of his horse's companionship. They'd been logging alone together for seven years in the Knapp Pond woodlands.

In his seventh year of confinement with no visitors, an older con encouraged Clem to go to work in the woodshop making desks for the new state office building to help pass the time. Over the ensuing years, Clem lost track of the number of desks he'd made, but after a few years, he got permission to make birdhouses. These soon became the hit of the shop crew. All the prison guards had several at their homes. Under the watchful eye of the shop foreman, Clem made finch houses, bluebird nesting boxes, and ornate purple martin houses. Word of his birdhouses spread beyond the prison walls, and townsfolk asked to buy his work. But prisoners were not allowed to sell their handicrafts or to receive money, so Clem got permission to sell all the houses he could make through the Windsor Methodist Church, which agreed to donate the money to the local 4-H group.

Every time I visit Clem, he confides in me his fear of leaving. His greatest concern is losing access to his shop and tools.

"Hain't been on the outside since I's twenty-five. Hell, don't even know what it looks like out there. All I can see from my cell is the heavens, and I sure as hell ain't gonna end up there after what I done. Sometimes I sees an' hears an aeroplane. I coun't ever 'just to th'outside. All I got's my birdhouses and dovecotes. How'm I gonna make 'em on the outside wi' no tools or such?"

I talk with corrections and a judge in Superior Court and offer to pro-vide transitional housing, taking Clem into the rectory for the time being with no idea of what will become of him after that. I've been his only con-sistent visitor for the last six years, and I have two open bedrooms now that Clarisse has had to move in with Ma and Cecil found work on a Barre Public Works roadcrew and moved into a small apartment.

On the day I'm to pick up Clem, they let me inside rather than just leave him standing at the main entrance, as they ordinarily do with outgoing prisoners. This way I can help him pack up his few things and be with him as he says goodbye to his few friends and correction officers, several of whom are trying to hide their own tears on seeing him leave. Forty-eight years is a long time to live in a tiny space with few friends, and I wonder if it was the best use of society's money.

As a boy, I saw the impulsive nature of immature young men all the time and later, as a priest, I hear about it weekly in the confessional. I have to believe there's a better path to manhood than spending most of one's life in a cage for an act of impulsive rage. The many young male aggressors I've known either escaped punishment through privilege or forgiveness, or they were condemned for their immaturity to a life of atoning for one bad choice. If I'm fallible in the eyes of God, I may be forgiven — not so in the eyes of my peers. Society offers no absolution and little rehabilitation. Sometimes I lose track of who's the sinner.

I walk Clem outside the prison walls. He shields his eyes from the bright sun as we walk towards my VW. Clem has seen very few cars except in magazines. He's nervous but curious as he settles into the passenger side. I see his hand caressing the dashboard and seat fabrics. He seems to be humming to himself. We drive to the rectory in silence as he takes in the sights and sounds he hasn't seen in forty-eight years. Driving through Windsor, he suddenly shouts, "There's one a' my birdhouses. I made that there. I reco'nize it. I made it. Looks good don' it."

I acknowledge his enthusiasm. As we drive, he scans the village he hasn't seen since his trial.

"There's where I 'as tried, the courthouse. I forgets what it looked like, 'though I seen it in some 'a my dreams when the policemens brought me out and everyone in town was shouting and yelling for me to be 'anged. Probably should 'a been for what I done. Not a day goes by I don't rue it. Bastard pained my horse for life but didn't deserved what I done ta 'im.

"This yer house, Father Pierre? Nice house. 'Is where I'll be stayin' 'til I finds someplace else?"

"You're welcome to stay as long as you need, Clem, and we're gonna set you up a woodshop in the garage. I never use it. They say cars last longer if you leave 'em out in the winter anyway; they say they don't rust as fast."

I walk Clem into the rectory and his eyes go to the ornate wood-work, furniture, and rugs, which are alien to him.

"Seen places like 'is in magazines but never in life. You live 'ere long?"

"The rectory belongs to the parish, not me. This is hardly a life-style I'd choose, but the Church had money in the days when this was built. Now, it can barely afford to heat its churches. I like this place though 'cause I can take in friends. I've had several since I moved in. I live here now with Clarisse who takes care of my mother who suffers from dementia. We get along well enough. You'll see."

I show Clem his room. "It's too big," is his first reaction. "I do'an need 'is much space, too big I tell ya."

"It's all I've got, Clem. You'll get used to it. Settle in and make yourself at home. The bathroom is down the hall on the right. If the door's shut, it means Ma or Clarisse is in there. If it's open, you can go in. There's a bath and shower you can use any time. If either of them has used the bath, you may have to wait ten minutes for the water to reheat. The system's a little slow to recover.

"Why don't you unpack your things and lie down? It's been a big day."

Standing at the window, Clem seems not to have heard me.

"Lots'a birds out there. Have to build 'em some houses. Don't want 'em laying their eggs where it ain't safe. Funny, I never seen who lives in all 'em houses I built over the years."

I close the door quietly and leave Clem to settle in.

In anticipation of his leaving prison, I've asked my parishioners to drop off any unused woodworking tools in the garage. A retired Italian carpenter made Clem a woodworking bench, and I used a collection plate of cash destined for the bishop's Fund several months back to buy Clem a power jigsaw. It's all set up in the garage and I'll show it to him tomorrow after breakfast.

Ma

The chaos and fear in Ma's head is overwhelming her voluntary responses and now attacking her involuntary body functions like swallowing and breathing. Clarisse warns me that the end is near. I see, too, that Clarisse is exhausted from feeding and cleaning Ma and having to watch her every move.

My understanding of dementia is, like so many things in my life, vicarious. I've heard confessions wherein an ashamed caregiver confesses their resentment towards a beloved parent, child, or relative who is wholly dependent on them for care. A Methodist minister I came to know, who also frequented Windsor Prison, once advised me to pay as much, if not more, attention to the caregiver than to those they care for, as the caregiver can't look forward to the peace that death will bring the person they're caring for. I didn't understand this at the time but do now, as I watch Clarisse spend every waking moment and much of the time she should be sleeping attending to Ma.

I try to give her occasional breaks but that just means I sit with Ma, while Clarisse takes a nap or tries to catch up with her own life, until Ma begins crying or screaming or soils herself and her bed-clothes, and I know only to ask for Clarisse's help.

I watch one day as she gives Ma a sponge bath and light alcohol rub. Clarisse no longer bathes Ma in the bathtub, as Ma's become terrified of being in water. I watch as Clarisse tenderly strokes Ma's pale naked limbs up and down. Ma's translucent skin drapes loosely over her skeletal frame. How is it I've never seen or experienced such tenderness? Clarisse is humming a lullaby softly to Ma as she applies the cooling alcohol. I'm no longer embarrassed to see Ma's nakedness and, for the first time, see her person apart from her sex.

At Clarisse's suggestion, I call Dr. Huebner and ask him to come and do an assessment of Ma. Lucienne agrees to take some sick leave and join me for the consult. I can no longer leave this to Clarisse. Dr. Huebner explains to Clarisse, Lucienne, and me that Ma will die in a few weeks either of choking, heart failure, or suffocation and that we will not be able to manage her death alone. He recommends moving her to a hospital in Barre, where the final stage of her disease can be better managed.

An ambulance comes the following day, and two orderlies remove Ma, screaming, from the room she's known since she came to live with me. I can see the look of terror and betrayal on her face. An orderly whispers to me that Ma doesn't even know me, that for dementia patients any change is terrifying. He promises to sedate her in the ambulance and assures me they will take good care of her. She's strapped to a gurney and wheeled out into the sunshine. I watch as the orderlies collapse the gurney's steel legs to load her into the ambulance. Oddly, I'm reminded of watching cranes take off from the seacoast in New Hampshire and how, when airborne, they fold their long gangly legs into their chest feathers.

Ma looks at me puzzled as they slide her into the ambulance. I turn away. Clarisse gives Ma a kiss and puts her arm around me, pulling me toward her. I'm not aware of it, but she tells me later I was crying. I know myself so poorly. Was it out of sadness, knowing this is the last time I'd see Ma alive or out of gratitude for Clarisse's understanding and kindness?

That night, I sleep fitfully and wake up in the middle of the night to find Clarisse in my bed. She's turned away from me and sleeping peacefully. I get up to use the john. When I return, Clarisse whispers to me, "I hope it's okay. I couldn't sleep in that room with Elise gone. I knew I'd never sleep."

I'm at a loss for words; she senses this and whispers, "It's okay, I just need sleep."

I soon hear her breathing softly.

I go back to sleep after some time, realizing I'm grateful for her company and that she's asked nothing of me. We're simply two people in the warmth of a shared bed.

Clarisse and I visit Ma two days later. She looks peaceful in her starched white sheets, her head barely making a dent in the firm pillow. When we greet her, she doesn't recognize us and turns her attention back to the child's mobile hung above her bed which seems to fascinate her with its drifting colored panels.

Clarisse senses my sadness and takes my hand. I tear up. I've absolved so many of my parishioners of their guilt, but always feared comforting them with my touch. Clarisse sees me trying to hide my sadness and confusion and whispers, "It's all right."

Ma dies the following week. Lucienne and Clarisse promise to help me organize the funeral. I'll be the celebrant of a funeral Mass "for the repose of the soul of Elise Carrier," as it's posted in the church bulletin. This is all I'm capable of.

With no discussion, Clarisse continues to share my bed. She's usually in bed sleeping peacefully when I arrive in my shabby pajamas. We sleep fully clothed and, in time, feel comfortable moving closer to one another. I awake one morning with Clarisse's arm over my back. She's fast asleep. Her exhalations generate a gentle sound, reminding me of the barely audible sound of the old church tracker organ as its electric bellows blew air through its reeds and pipes when no stops had been pulled or keys struck.

The shared loneliness and sadness that has us sharing my bed has come to feel natural to me, though I know it jeopardizes my legitimacy in the eyes of my parishioners and my Church. I know Clarisse and I should discuss this but I'm afraid of losing her affection and company.

Clem doesn't seem to notice. Like mine, his life experience is so circumscribed that he probably thinks nothing of our sharing a bed. In our many conversations, Clem made clear he was never a church-goer and expressed no interest in ever becoming one.

Lake Groton

One Sunday after Mass — a time we usually keep open for relaxation and a meal shared with our boarders — Clarisse suggests we drive north to Lake Groton and have a picnic. She blows the dust off an old wicker picnic hamper from the pantry, stocks it with cheese and pickle sandwiches, and fills its dented thermos with a lemonade she makes from fresh-squeezed lemons and an orange for sweetness. I'm surprised by her initiative and suppress my instinct to stay home.

Driving north through the no-man's-land between Barre and Groton, I feel an unfamiliar sense of relief and happiness. The weather's clear and I have no obligations until Mass the following morning.

I'm struck by the extraordinary poverty of the landscape through which we're driving. I see dwellings and animal shelters fashioned out of old semi-trailers, plywood crates, listing mobile homes, inhabited cellar holes, and farmhouses with plastic sheeting over broken windows. I saw suburban poverty as a child but nothing like this.

"Who cares for these people?" I ask Clarisse.

"Slow down after the crest of the hill," Clarisse says without answering my question.

We round a wide curve and begin a steep descent that follows a roiling river on our left.

"You see that log-truck run-away lane over there to the right? Pull in and off to the side. They're not used anymore. Logging operations ended here when this became a state park." I do as she asks, pulling into the turn-off.

Clarisse seems to be looking for something in the distance. I see nothing indicating any civilization. She opens the door and gets out. I follow her as she walks into the woods, picking her way along an overgrown path that parallels the road on which we've been traveling. We walk a few hundred yards along this path overgrown with blackberry bushes and young ash trees. I hear the occasional car passing by on the road off to our left.

We arrive at a clearing overgrown with woody lilac bushes just coming into bloom. Behind them, I see the remains of a house. It resembles so many of the rural houses I've seen — a symmetrical façade with two windows on each floor on either side of the front door. A fieldstone slab lies beneath the entrance. The first-story windows are all broken. A crumbling chimney leans away from the right side of the house, looking as if it might fall at any minute. The front door is ajar. The former lawn is overgrown with brambles, errant lilac, sumac and alder shoots, and two barren apple trees with countless water shoots pointing skyward like a flight of arrows ready to launch. A collapsed barn lies comfortably on itself, and an ancient tractor rusts in the shade of a dying butternut. The rear wheels are iron with cast diagonal treads. The cast-iron tractor seat is missing, "probably taken by some hunter to make a bar stool," mutters Clarisse.

I'm at a loss as to why Clarisse has brought me here. A stranger to the woods I'm struck by the silence that reminds me of the chapel at St. John's. All I can hear is Clarisse's footsteps breaking small twigs as she looks around in what she explains to me was the front yard of her childhood home.

I know not to ask questions, and, suddenly, we're walking back to the car. Clarisse gets in, tears streaming down her face. It's cool and the sun's out. At first, I thought it was perspiration, as I, too, was damp from our walk, but there's no moisture on her forehead, only in the swale between her cheeks and upper lip. I know she is deep in herself. After shifting into fourth gear, I reach out and take her hand as she looks away out the side window.

Clarisse daubs at her cheek with her sleeve and shortly thereafter points to a large log sign indicating the entrance to Groton State Park. She whispers directions to me until we arrive at a rocky shoreline marked "Groton Lake Public Access." A fisherman is busy launching his aluminum boat while his son and daughter ferry tackle, bait boxes, and picnic fare into the boat from their station wagon. Together they push the boat into the water, hopping in as it takes float. The father begins fussing with the small teal-colored outboard and soon, in a cloud of blue smoke, the entourage putts off along the heavily treed shoreline.

Clarisse heads out along a path that follows the opposite shore. The path is varicosed with the exposed root systems and occasional vein of protruding granite. After picking our way along the well-worn path, Clarisse climbs up on a massive boulder overhung by a triad of white birches bending down toward the water.

"This is my spot," she announces setting the picnic hamper down and offering me a hand.

"Like many other ponds and lakes in this region," she explains, "Groton Lake was chiseled out during the glacial recession, and these boulders are all that's left." The sadness is gone from her demeanor and voice, and she seems genuinely glad to be here.

"It's beautiful here. Did you come here as a child?"

"Yes, my sister and I would ride our bikes the three miles from home to the lake and then come out here to 'our rock,' as we called it. My parents knew only that we were going to the lake to swim." I sit down next to her as she unpacks our sandwiches and thermos.

I ask what happened to their home. She looks away toward the opposite shore.

"We lost it to the bank when I was eleven. Pa drank. He tried every sort of work, but the drink always lost him his job. Uncle Reggie moved in with us to help Ma but soon he was messing with me and Hélène. We couldn't get away from him. Pa was never home, and Ma didn't believe us, so we ran away but were returned home by a neighbor who saw us walking along the highway at dusk. Uncle Reggie told us if we told anyone that we'd be put in jail and would never be able to marry and have children of our own. At ten and thirteen, we didn't know any better.

"The second time we ran away, we were picked up by the police. They suspected something and sent someone to the house. Ma was hysterical, but the policeman calmed her down, and Ma confessed she'd suspected all along but could never admit to herself what Uncle Reggie was doing to us.

Nothing ever happened to him, but Hélène and I were removed from our house and put into foster care. We heard much later that Uncle Reggie and Ma had taken off. We never heard from Pa again, and to this day, I've no idea what happened to him. He was a kind man and would never have let Uncle Reggie do the things he did to us, but he was so hampered by drink he could never make anything work."

She is looking at the opposite shore. I put my arm around her shoulder and draw her to myself. To my astonishment, she suddenly stands up, sheds her clothes in a pile, and dives naked into the pond, barely making a splash. Surfacing a few yards out, she swims to the middle, turns around and returns, all in a few minutes. Rising out of the water dripping, she climbs back onto the rock, dries herself off with the checkered table cloth, and dons her clothes. I notice the water drops sparkling in the sun on her dark pubic hair. She interrupts my gaze saying only "Baptism."

Never let religion upend your spiritual life

Our life together in the rectory is comfortable. Several times, I ask Clarisse after we've retired to my bedroom if she wants to talk about her family and her homelife, and each time she shakes her head and remains silent.

Clem is happiest in the garage, where he spends most of his days. At his advanced age, he now naps after our lunch together, and then returns enthusiastically to his work. At supper, he's gotten chattier about his work and the "'culiar folk who stop by ta look 'n buy." When he first moved in, he was virtually mute, so his new-found voice is refreshing. Even though the small town of Graniteville is full of his work, the demand continues unabated, and a craft shop in nearby Montpelier gives Clem a standing order for all he can produce as long as each piece is unique.

Clarisse's residence is noted by community members, some of whom have come to believe she's a housekeeper. Some older priests have live-in older cooks and an occasional cleaning lady. Clarisse seems to have been accepted for now, even though she's still in her mid-40s.

I no longer masturbate and have no desire to, even though our new-found comfort with one another is uncomplicated by sex. I'd assumed that a man and woman sleeping in the same bed always had sex and am grateful simply to hold Clarisse close, feel her warmth and hear her breathing next to my chest. Clarisse confides in me that she cannot be touched intimately without recalling the specter of her uncle.

I struggle more than ever now to accommodate my faith. The rote words I recite in the seven Masses a week I offer now seem bleached of meaning, except for the tender *Agnus Dei* litany with its final *Dona nobis pacem* and the even briefer Greek *Kyrie Eleison*, a petition for mercy. Both retain their power for me in their profound humility.

The Church's recent abandonment of the Latin language in favor of colloquial English removed any mystery from the litany, replacing it with clunky language alien to my ears and to those of my few ageing parishioners who still attend Mass. The new language of the sacraments sounds more to me like someone reading the directions for a kitchen appliance.

I always regretted that we Catholics don't sing hymns. I was jealous of Paolo's community who celebrated the hours daily in plainsong. The few old English hymns I heard in interfaith celebrations always appealed to me in their baroque language and simple melodies. When music finally returned to the Catholic liturgy, it wasn't the solemn beauty of the hours I so loved at St. John's, but rather insipid folksy harmony sung by nuns with out-of-tune guitars, singing trite inanities.

I've grown weary of the hide-bound faith I was trained in. Listening to sinners elicits in me not the judgments of my lapsed faith but an affection and empathy for them that seems alien to my religious education. I must write Paolo.

Dear Paolo,

   Again, I am sorry for my long silence. I wish we were closer to one another. I am writing to ask if you've retained the faith we studied at St. John's. I must confess mine has all but abandoned me. I rarely pray any more for faith or for the intercession of the Saints. I pray occasionally out of fear and doubt, but my prayers are generic. I don't know to whom I am praying or for what. My usual prayer is: "Oh Lord, please be in me and with me." But I no longer know who this Lord is, if he is listening, or why he would even care to hear from me. It's like I'm praying into an abyss.

I discharge my ecclesiastical duties like an automaton, sometimes even skipping parts of the Mass I'm supposed to read to myself. The Mass has become like a ghost dance I do for the few people left in my pews. I'm convinced that if the bishop wasn't so desperate for vocations in his diocese, I'd have been counselled out of the priesthood long ago. I know he's gotten complaints from a couple in my parish whose daughter and fiancé I married a few months ago.

In the service, I asked them if they took one another etc., etc. and when each said, "I do," I told them they'd "married one another and that I was honored to witness their ceremony." They looked perplexed, as I'd omitted some of the nuptial liturgy, saying instead, "You've joined yourselves together in marriage. May you love one another long and well and may your family and community be there to support you in your love." Then I motioned to them to recess down the aisle to their waiting family and friends. I could see from the altar the concerned whispers and nods at the back of the church and returned to the rectory.

As I mentioned in my last letter, Ma died, and her devoted caregiver Clarisse stayed on and now shares my bed, not as you might imagine, but as a dear friend and confidant. I've never experienced tenderness, having always confused it with sex.

If I missed my faith, I'd seek spiritual counsel and pray to restore it, but I've simply come to believe that much of religion — ours and those of others — is little more than the artifice of our male fancies. I've come to fear that its damage to humankind has too often outweighed its good.

I told you about Father Arthur's study of the Church's fascination with torture and the subjugation of women as evil sirens. I see examples in all religions of men using their faith to subjugate and persecute women. Church history is rife with slaughter in its aggregation of wealth and power.

The liberation theologists of South and Central America, whom we studied and discussed, seem as close to anything spiritual as the Church could ever muster but they are still condemned by Rome. Many, like Archbishop Romero, were simply murdered for following in Christ's footsteps.

Having so thoroughly lost my way among our own and the world's religions, I still value the cohesive power of our small New England churches, whose members watch over and care for one another. It's only when that attention becomes surveillance and judgment that the dark side of religion again rears its ugly head. It seems we will always have among us fearful and insecure people who resist spiritual exploration and change — their only way of defining themselves against some perceived external evil. Empathy comes hard to these people.

The penances I now dispense are rarely prayers anymore but works. I ask those whom I'm about to absolve to do something in our town for someone in need rather than just kneeling at the altar rail intoning Hail Marys. I may ask a penitent to bring a meal to someone whom I know is sick or visit a dying member of our parish. Most seem to appreciate the chance to do good works, although some ask me outright, "Can't I just say a rosary?"

*Increasingly, my "absolutions" include my asking parish-
ioners to forgive themselves and one another, something long
missing from the Sacrament of Penance. I assure them that God
will forgive them if they can also forgive themselves and each
other. Most of my parishioners seem content with this, but there
a few who resent my departure from the familiar liturgy.*

*I spend more of my time in prison ministry. My horror at the
crimes committed by the men I visit is moderated by my growing
affection for them. I'm learning to distinguish the crime from
the criminal — to detest the crime but love the criminal. As I
get to know them better, I've come to understand how misery
perpetuates itself through the generations. Abuse cultivates
further abuse. I can do little for these men other than listen to
them and bring small bits of communication to their families.
I've managed to reconcile several offenders with their families
and, in a few cases, their victims, which brings me great satis-
faction and them a safe path home.*

*I hope you will understand how much I cherish our friend-
ship, even as it has become epistolary. I am eager for news of
you and your life in the monastery. Please write and assure me
of your love, as I do you mine.*

Your Brother,

Pierre

Fra Pierre,

*I am so glad to hear from you and to know you are well.
Your loss of faith comes as no surprise. Although my life and
faith took a very different course, I have experienced much the
same growth in my own spiritual life. I suppose it is a judgment
to refer to "the loss of one's faith" as spiritual growth. It's a topic*

we often discuss here, and Doubting Thomas comes up in our discussion. I have a reprint of Caravaggio's "The Incredulity of St. Thomas" in my cell, which you must try to see. You can find it in your library in any book on Caravaggio. The painting is fundamental to my faith, for I have come to realize that faith without doubt is meaningless, just as courage without threat is not courage. As my father-confessor often says to me, "Never let your religion derail your spiritual life."

I'm happy living among my brethren. Our community is diverse, and I am not close to everyone, but the compression of monastic life necessarily reduces judgment and conflict. I'm in a relationship as well with Fra Lindner. We're celibate by choice, as you are in your friendship with Clarisse. Our affection for one another no longer necessitates the physical. This is the case with many brothers. The rigidity of our daily ritual precludes the warmth of proximity that you and Clarisse enjoy. I am jealous. Sometimes, I just yearn to be held.

My breads have become more than a source of sustenance for the abbey, as they are now sold daily in our small shop, along with our condiments and cheeses. Brother Lindner is experimenting with our orchardist on an eau de vie not unlike the calvados we sometimes shared in the evenings at St. John's. As you requested earlier, I will arrange to have a small package of the fruits of our labor sent to you. My black Russian bread is everyone's current favorite, and it keeps well for several weeks.

Much love,
Yours in perpetual doubt,
Fra Paolo

The Bishop's Displeasure

I just received a warning letter from the bishop. I'm now so distanced from Church doctrine and mandates that I barely noticed the diocesan return address and seal on the letterhead. If I were to be defrocked at this stage of my life, what would I become, a prison guard? I've long since forgiven the few in my parish who attend Mass simply to monitor and report my latest transgressions to the bishop.

His letter reiterates his earlier concerns about my diverging from the sacramental liturgy, "as recorded in the 1956 Benziger Edition of the *New Roman Missal* by Father Lasance under the imprimatur of Francis Cardinal Spellman D.D. and approved by the Holy See." I ignore the legalese at my peril and read on.

The bishop reports having received word that I'm administering sacraments to two divorced and remarried women in my parish who have not requested or received a formal declaration of nullity for their first marriage, although he doesn't allude to the several divorced and re-married men to whom I also offer communion. He says he's heard, but cannot confirm, that I've absolved a young girl who had an abortion, re-minding me that abortion is a mortal sin commensurate with murder.

Under the new protocols of *Vatican II*, he reminds me, only bish-ops can absolve the sin of abortion. He further alludes to the presence of an ex-convict in the rectory but says he'll rely on my judgment as to the propriety of that arrangement. He says he also understands a woman is living in the rectory and asks my assurance that she is merely a "domestic," and that there's "nothing untoward" about her residence there. He asks for a response to his questions by return mail. I toss the letter in the wastebasket and finish my coffee, which is now cold.

I know I must reconcile my loss of faith and my vocation as a parish priest with the bishop's expectations if I'm to continue to reside here and minister to my parishioners, who seem, for the most part, to like me despite my eccentricities.

Clarisse is making a pilgrimage to Groton Lake with a friend, so I arrange to visit the prison and set out early in the morning. Offenders are given notice of my visit and can request a half-hour's counselling session with me. For many, these meetings have supplanted the perfunctory confessions and communions.

As I drive up, I'm still daunted by the sheer cubic volume of concrete and red brick that confines this graveyard of living humanity. The elevated searchlight and machine gun turrets at each corner and the serpentine coils of barbed wire topping the fourteen-foot walls remind me, each time I come, of society's collective fear and judgment of the sometimes gentle and broken men I meet inside.

I go to my usual "Interview Room 4" and await my first visitor. Jack, the corrections officer who usually oversees my prison visits, ushers in Freddie, a wary old con who seems to like my visits simply to have someone to talk to. Freddie's not seeking salvation, just the comfort of someone who will listen to his feelings about the lifetime of wrongs that landed him here. As I listen to Freddie, I wonder what Ma would think of me sitting here. She would have fretted about my safety, whereas Pa would have judged me crazy, as he had little sympathy for the mistakes of others.

Freddie begins bragging again about his misdeeds. When he sees my lack of admiration and I ask him how he felt about them, his first response is, "Made me a livin'. Fed my fambly good enough. Wasn't all bad." He then answers my pointed question as to how he felt about stealing and hurting others, and he breaks down. He lowers his head and talks perceptively about the people he hurt. Freddie is sorry for what he's done, and he ends our discussions with, "Wish I could take it all back, didn't know not to hurt some'un so bad. Din't know no better… learn't most of what I know from Da, who could be a mean bastard. As a kid, I al'ays hated mean. Don't know how I got to be so mean m'self… wish I could take it back, but I done it and I'm here for another eight years by my reckonin', but I lose track a' time. Seems like there's only days in here, not years or such. Glad you came, Father Pierre." Freddie stands and turns away from me as Jack cuffs him and escorts him back to his cell.

Next, Jack brings in a new offender whom I've never met. His name is Alphonse, and he's serving ten years for car theft, involuntary manslaughter, drunk driving/death resulting, and resisting arrest — a familiar litany of charges associated with lifelong alcoholism. My years of hearing confessions about the sinful results of alcoholic binges — sexual indiscretions, car accidents, fistfights, shoplifting, theft — leaves me confused not about the sins themselves but about where the "sin" resides. Is the sin the alcohol addiction itself or its drink-induced behaviors?

If, as we were taught, sin must be a conscious, knowing, and free act of evil, does it lie in the alcoholic's failure to abstain from his addiction or in the "diminished responsibility" of alcoholic-induced wreckage? This question haunts me, especially as I hear more medical experts defining alcoholism as an addiction requiring medical intervention rather than criminal punishment. They challenge the idea that alcoholism is a moral failing, and I've come pretty much to the same conclusion just from the number of alcoholic priests I've come to know over my years.

My first mentor, Father Conran, was by his own admission an alcoholic, even, as he so often told me, after he quit drinking, which I have only recently come to understand. So how do we judge the transgressions that occur under alcohol's influence?

Alf sits quietly in the folding chair, stares at his hands, and says nothing. I ask him why he sought my company. "Dunno," he mutters. "Jess wanted to see someone, I guess. I done wrong but di'nt mean ta. Kill't a young girl riding her bike. I 'as drunk, but that ain' no excuse, I know. Wanted ta kill myself afterwards. She died in my arms and she was lookin' at me, all scared like. I can't ever forget her face. Din't leave the accident 'til she 'as dead. Could a been my own daughter. Never could live with myself after'ards. Tried to kill myself with drink but ended up here only a few months later. Serving a life sentence. I'll die here."

Alf begins sobbing quietly. "I still see her, but I mix up her face and my daughter's. Never saw my fambly again… too ashamed I was. Never want to. I better get back. I'm on laundry detail and lose privileges if I'm late. Thanks for seeing me. Do'an know what I 'spected."

I ask Alf to sit back down. He does.

"Do you want to spend the rest of your life here?" I ask him.

"I'd like to see my daughters again, but ain' sure I could face 'em if they knew what I done. Parole Board says I might come up for compassion release if the victim's a'vocate can get agreement from the girl I kil't's fambly."

"When's the parole hearing?" I ask.

"Next month. But I don't know nothin' 'bout no victim's a'vocate, nor how ta talk to 'em… all beyon' me."

With that, he rises and is cuffed by Jack and led away.

My final visitor is a scapegrace named Luther. Our visits are usually brief and mostly transactional. Luther never doubts his own innocence. Charged with physically and sexually abusing his wife, Martha, Luther is a detainee awaiting trial. In his mind, I've unwittingly become his link to her. He seems both to love her and resent her for bringing charges against him.

"Tell Martha ta talk to my defense lawyer again and ask about gettin' these foolish charges dropped, would'ja? Hope the state don't pay 'im much, he sure 'nough don't earn his pay, workin' for me anyhow."

I try to reason with Luther about why his wife turned him in for landing her in the emergency room with a concussion, broken wrist, and two broken ribs, but he dismisses her reaction as bad judgment. "She din't mean it. She loves me the way I am. Some bitch named Rena talked her into layin 'em charges agin me. Martha gets easily 'suaded by 'er."

Luther sees Martha largely as chattel with bad judgment. He wants to be back with her but will, I'm convinced, beat her senseless again if he's released for having turned him in. He can't believe she doesn't love him or want him back.

Martha lives in nearby Williamstown and I've visited her twice. The chasm between her terror of Luther's violence and wish to be safe from him, and his firm belief in her abiding love is unbridgeable. I ask Luther if he was ever beaten up as a kid by an older, stronger boy.

"Wa'nt never beat up by no kid, but Pa used to beat me and Ma when we done wrong. If Ma cooked sompin' Pa din't like, he'd punish her good for it. If I skipped out on my chores stackin' wood, he'd beat me. We 'spected it. How else ya gonna learn?"

I'm at a loss. I don't know how to tell him that Martha never wants to see him again and feels safe for the first time in her life as long as he's behind bars.

"Thanks for comin'. Do'n forgets to tell that asshole defense 'ttorney to get on my case and tell Martha I'll see her soon." With that he rises and is cuffed by Jack, who has overheard the whole encounter and just shakes his head.

"Some people don't ever get it," he whispers to me as he leads Luther away.

Driving home in a pelting rain, I have no idea what to tell Martha other than to see to her own safety. I won't convey any of Luther's message to her but will urge her to find a safe place where he can never find her again.

My mind wanders as I drive through the pelting rain. So often my faith has been complicit in the idea of women as chattel. The Church's history inspires no confidence in me that it sees women as equal beings in the eyes of God. I recall the bishop's letter, in which he accuses me of "providing spiritual cover to women who in the Church's eyes can no longer receive the sacraments because they've contravened Church doctrine and live in a state of perpetual sin."

I suddenly recall Father Conran's sermon on Mary Magdalene. What inspired Pope Gregory to deliver a sermon changing her legacy from virgin to harlot, or Tomás de Torquemada to incinerate so many women in the Inquisition? Why has one of the great spiritual, artistic, and scientific scholars of the Middle Ages, Hildegard of Bingen, been denied sainthood for the last thousand years? Most of the Church's women saints were either martyrs or mothers of male saints. Do women have a place in my Church, other than as child bearers, rummage sellers, or nuns? Clarisse and I talk about this and she's clear, "they don't," she says. Women can't be priests and must "honor" their husbands. I find nothing in the life of Christ that justifies the Church's view of women.

Clarisse is home and seems refreshed from her journey to Groton Lake. She's full of the energy and the lightness she radiates after a swim at "her rock." She prepares us a supper of chicken braised in wine, onion, tomatoes and fresh oregano, and with great ceremony, opens a bottle of *Lachryma Christi del Vesuvio,* a wine she found in Montpelier, knowing I'd enjoy the peculiar name of its label. We share a rapturous meal, small talk of my prison visit and her recall of the loons she saw nesting on Groton Lake and later heard calling to one another as she drove off.

Alf Joins Our Home

I'm haunted by my discussion with Alf, his anxiety about leaving the security of prison and his wish to see his daughters before he dies. So often I see the entropy of shame consume the will to live. Alf is harmless to society and content to die behind bars but wants to see his daughters again, despite his shame.

The following day, I decide to contact the victim's advocate but have no more knowledge of that person's office than Alf does, so I call the warden with whom I've become friends. He's unavailable, but his secretary explains the new role of victim advocate to me. I'd assumed that this office would automatically support the victim's understandable sense of loss, grief, and vengefulness so many crime victims feel but was pleased to hear that the role is more mediative, ensuring that the family's wishes and feelings are heard and respected and that those of a contrite offender are communicated to and considered by the victim and their family. I'm given the name and number of a Victoria Roy and call her to learn more. She lives in Montpelier, and we agree to meet for coffee the following day.

I spend the rest of my afternoon in the confessional. I've become adept at knowing whether my parishioner simply wants a perfunctory absolution and a ticket to heaven or whether they want spiritual guidance, for which I prefer a rectory visit to save the time of those in church lined up for their celestial ticket.

Back at the rectory, I see a note from Clarisse saying she's gone shopping, so I make us a modest supper of pasta, into which I shake a jar of spaghetti sauce. I toast some garlic bread and make a tasteless salad of iceberg lettuce and Russian dressing from a bottle in the fridge. Like my faith, my cooking skills are weak. Clarisse brings joy to her cooking, making her own flavorful sauces and dressings but is gracious about my dismal culinary skills.

We talk about Groton Lake again. I've come to understand its meaning in her life and am envious of how alive that granite rock is to her. My space was the chapel at St John's, in which I often dream myself, both alone and with Paolo, but always in silence lit by evening light flowing in from the clerestory windows high above.

I suggest we camp at Lake Groton for a few days before fall sets in. She welcomes the idea and gives me a hug as I wash up the two dishes she clears from the table.

The next day, I meet Miss Roy in a diner in Montpelier. She's a vibrant young woman, not at all what I expected from the criminal justice community. We settle into a cramped booth: me with my milky coffee and she with her black tea. I tell her of my visit with Alf and his ambivalence about leaving prison and his desire to see his daughters before he dies.

Having heard from the parole board with a request for her input on their decision whether to grant Alf parole, she has visited the surviving mother of the girl Alf killed in the accident. Recently widowed, she has retired from nursing and spoke freely with Miss Roy about her continuing sense of loss. Miss Roy reported that she was thoughtful, especially in her capacity to differentiate between her enduring anger at those who drive drunk, alluding to the carnage she saw daily in the emergency room, and the courage of those who commit to recovery, and seek forgiveness for the damage they've done under alcohol's influence.

She said was weary of mourning her loss but would rather not meet the driver who killed her daughter. She offered to write a letter supporting parole for the prisoner, whose name she'd forgotten. For reasons of confidentiality, Miss Roy explains, she cannot tell me her client's name, and I remind her, as a father-confessor, I understand. She smiles warmly.

Several days later, I again make the trip to Windsor to talk with Alf and to let him know that his victim's mother and only surviving relative won't oppose his parole. He seems surprised at this information.

"She do'n' still hate me?" he asks. "I kilt her only daughter."

"I'm sure she misses her daughter every day, but people do forgive, Alf, and life goes on. Think you can ever forgive yourself?"

"I done it. I live with it ever' day, but I'd like to see my girls 'afore I die. They'se womens now, but still. Last time I saw 'em, 'ey was little girls. My brother raised 'em up, so I heard."

"The girl's mother's forgiven you; God's forgiven you. It's time for you to forgive yourself, go to your bail hearing, and say the right things. You know what they are. Your case manager will ask about housing; I have a room left in the rectory where you can stay till you get your feet under you.

Remember Clem, the old guy who made birdhouses? He's been living with me since he got out. Maybe he could offer you some work. At 89, he's got more than he can handle. I'll tell the parole board, you have a place to go and possible employment if they'll grant you parole."

"Think I'd ever find my girls?" Alf asked. "S'been a lot a' years."

"I know we can find them, if they're still around. You worry about getting ready for your bail hearing and I'll write a letter to the warden, telling him I can give you a place to stay. Take care now. It'll be okay."

I leave Alf as Jack returns. He no longer cuffs Alf, just leads him off to his cell.

The following week, I write a letter on parish stationery, confirming that I will provide Alf with transitional housing and counselling, as needed.

Seven weeks later, Alf's case is heard, and I get a certified letter from the parole board corrections saying that prisoner number 47729, Alphonse Rochefolle will be released from Windsor State Correctional facility on Friday, June 6th at 3:00 PM into my custody. I stare at the letter aghast. In my many years in the French-Canadian community, I've never seen the name *Rochefolle*, except after Clarisse's name

• • •

I'm at a loss. Clarisse is visiting a friend several houses down the street whom she's been caring for in her decline. She jokes that after Ma died, that she had no one to care for. So when an old friend with whom she's always gathered flowers in the spring woods comes down with multiple sclerosis and is wheelchair bound, Clarisse takes her out and pushes her through the woodland paths in her *chaise-roulante* as she calls it, as if it were a pet. Cécile's English is spotty, and it gives Clarisse a chance to keep up her French, of which she is proud.

Other than at our first trip to Groton Lake, Clarisse has never confided much to me about her family, nor have I pressed her on the subject, knowing from our discussion the depth of her fear and sadness as a young girl.

I can't be sure that Alphonse Rochefolle, whom I've invited unknowingly to share our home, is her father and am at a loss how to ask her. Had I known, I would have asked her before I offered him a room. I sink into the couch in the living room and, for the first time in a long time, think of asking God for counsel as I sip a scotch and tea.

I hear Clarisse coming into the kitchen with a cheery, "Allo, Pierre. You home?"

"In here…" I answer, "drinking," I say in a nervous attempt at humor.

"I'll pour a glass of Christ's tears and join you," she answers good-naturedly.

I hear the clink of glasses and Clarisse walks into the living room with a wine glass and a warm smile. I rise and offer her a hug.

"Aren't you loving today. What've I done to deserve such affection?" she laughs.

"I really love you," I answer sheepishly.

"I know you do, and I love you as well. You're a fine man, even though you're a priest," she says with an impish smile.

"I'm just not a very good priest," I respond.

I release her from my hug and step back. She senses my fear.

"Do you remember your father's name?" I ask.

"Of course, why do you ask?"

"What is it?" I ask.

"Why do you want to know?" she answers, now looking serious.

"What is it?" I repeat.

"You're serious," she says. "Alphonse René Rochefolle. Why are you asking me this? Did he die?"

"Sit down," I say.

"What's going on, please just tell me," Clarisse says, setting her wine on the side table.

"I had no idea who he was — just one of the many convicts I see in Windsor. At his request, I've been visiting him in prison. His age qualifies him for compassionate release by the parole board. He wanted to talk to someone outside about whether to ask for it or stay inside and serve out the rest of his life sentence. He's been in jail for a drunk-driving incident some thirty years ago that killed a young girl who died in his arms. I've never seen such a broken man. His remorse is like a cancer that's been consuming him in prison. We're only told offenders' first names. I knew him as Alf.

"The woman I met in Montpelier last week was a victim's advocate," a term new to me. She's been working with the girl's mother, even though the accident occurred decades ago, to determine whether she would oppose your father's early release.

"Having no idea of the relationship, I wrote to the parole board, recommending release and offering him transitional housing until he could get on his feet, thinking he could stay in the back room near the attic stairs. I didn't know he was your father. I'm so sorry."

Clarisse drops down into a chair and stares out the window.

I'm suddenly stricken with fear that Clarisse is angry and will leave. I walk over and take her hand.

"I'm sorry," I whisper.

"You did nothing wrong," she answers, still looking away. "You were just being your good self. Can we go to bed? I'm exhausted," she exhales.

I take her hand and we go to bed without supper. It's six-thirty.

The weather's turned warmer, and we lie fully clothed on top of the bed, holding one another as we so often do. I'm at a loss for words and know if there's anything to say, it's up to Clarisse. I've said enough.

Several times, she starts to say something, but then just stops and draws me closer, looking through me. I'm so relieved she's neither angry nor leaving. I chide myself again for my selfishness. The drama is hers, not mine. I'm merely an extra.

As the light dims outside. I fall asleep, aware that Clarisse is wide awake. Sometime later, I hear her ask me softly, "What does he look like, my father?"

I'm awake again and answer, "He's an old man. I don't know his age, but I imagine he's in his late sixties or early seventies, although he looks much older. I think the weight of his life and his years in prison have aged him. He talks fleetingly of having to leave his family, his drinking years, and then the accident, which broke his spirit.

"Did he mention my name?" Clarisse asked.

"He spoke only of his girls. You told me you had a sister, but you never told me any more. Is she around?"

"You never asked," Clarisse answered matter-of-factly, but implying no guilt.

"I'm asking now, if you want to talk about her," I answer.

"We separated many years ago. After we were taken from Ma and Uncle Richie and fostered out, the strangeness of our new family kept us very close, but we reacted differently to our fears. Hélène began to act out. I clammed up and just did whatever I was told by our new parents and by my teachers. I pretended to have no feelings at all. Hélène gave full vent to her fears and anger and was soon removed from the foster home, so I was now completely alone. My foster parents were nice enough and meant well, but their kindness could never break down the barriers I'd built around myself to stay safe or to quell the rage that Uncle Reggie's abuse had ignited in Hélène.

"I remember when the child welfare people came to take her away, I heard myself scream for the first time. It was like I'd suddenly become two people. I heard myself screaming at them not to take her away. My foster mother restrained me until Hélène was gone. I didn't come out of our room for three days. I wept and wept; I'd never felt so alone. Finally, I just resolved to survive. I'd survived Uncle Reggie, Pa's drinking, Ma's betrayal, and Hélène's removal. I was left with nothing but two kind foster parents to whom I couldn't relate.

"By eighteen, I'd graduated, found a job in a dry-cleaning plant, and rented my own room over a dry-goods store in town. I tried through child welfare to track down Hélène but was unable to. I was told only that she'd 'absconded,' but had no idea what that meant.

"Six years later, I married a boy in the dry-cleaning plant. We were married in his family's church. I think it was Congregational. I forget. He seemed nice enough, treated me respectfully, and I would even say he loved me. I found sex unbearable, however, but tolerated it for as long as I could. After eighteen months, I was pregnant. Denis was born, and I began to have new feelings I never thought possible.

"During most of my pregnancy, I thought I was sick, although I had no symptoms other than those associated with a first-time pregnancy. The growth of a child inside me brought me none of the joy I'd seen in other girls my age, even the ones who weren't married. Nothing about sex or pregnancy felt comfortable, but when Denis was born, things changed. Whatever maternal instincts lay dormant within me emerged. But Jacques wanted more children and I didn't. I began denying him sex and just after Denis turned two, Jacques took off with him, returning, as I later learned, to his family's farm in Ontario. I had no resources or desire to pursue him legally but missed Denis terribly. It felt like I'd simply lost another person in my life and that the succession of losses was my fault. Jacques and I never divorced, and I suspect he's remarried someone in Canada who will give him all the sex and children he wants.

"Several years later, I moved in here and began taking care of your Ma. Unable to care for myself, except in isolation, I took to caring for others, as it gave me a sense of being needed if not loved. But I've always lived in fear of being left alone again, as has happened so many times in my past."

"You never saw Hélène again?"

"I did, she showed up at my wedding to Jacques but left right after the service before we had any time together. Somehow, she'd heard I was getting married and just showed up. She looked terrible. She'd put on a lot of weight and drank heavily before and after the wedding. I wanted so much to talk to her, but the wedding service kept us apart, and after the small reception in the church basement, I looked all over for her, but she was gone. I never heard from her again. I'd do anything to see her. I'd like to bring her back to Groton Lake with me; she loved that rock as much as me."

I'm wide awake, listening intently. Clarisse is silent for a bit and then I hear the soft exhalations I associate with her sound sleep. I lie awake for several hours thinking of all I've just heard from the woman lying in my arms.

Confirmations

I'm preparing three young parishioners who've turned twelve in the last year for their confirmation and the bishop's visit. Priests do not generally administer the sacrament of confirmation in which young people become "Soldiers of Christ." It's my least favorite sacrament and one I could do entirely without. My patron saint, Martin of Tours, would never have approved of the Church's term, "Soldiers of Christ."

The bishop is scheduled to come in three weeks to draft his new soldiers into the Church's army, and I'm going through the hollow ritual of preparing them.

The following week I get a registered letter informing me that the bishop serving Vermont has retired "under difficult circumstances" and that my parish will be answering to a temporary parish administrator until a new bishop is appointed. It's increasingly evident that the dearth of priests is growing worse and that the Church is struggling to manage its dwindling parishes.

An article in the *Bennington Banner* soon confirms in print what's long been whispered. The Church's efforts to conceal its clergy's sexual abuse of children is now public, and for the first time, the Church is having to remove priests from parishes and turn them over to law enforcement for prosecution.

Clarisse's experience and the confessions I've heard on the subject make me realize how widespread child sexual abuse is both within and without the Church. I must now notify my students' parents their children will not soon be confirmed.

The shakeup serves me well, as the bishop's focus on my doctrinal deviations and my unusual living circumstances dissolves amid his dire legal circumstances.

There is no longer anyone to answer the letters from my few disgruntled parishioners.

A succession of grim diocesan news is followed by a letter from the diocesan administrator saying that my rectory is being put on the market but that, for now, my Graniteville church will be kept open, although there's talk of merging my parish with Barre. I will be given a living stipend and must find a place to move to in ninety days. I share this news with Clarisse who is still anxious about our planned trip next week to Windsor to pick up her father. Like me, she's not surprised by the Church's decision to sell the rectory.

Driving south to Windsor Prison to get Alf, I warn Clarisse what to expect, how the large prisoner exit door will roll sideways on its steel track, and her father will emerge alone for the first time in twenty-three years. Clarisse is quiet and looks out the window at the landscape scrolling by us.

"Are you nervous?" I ask.

Clarisse looks at me and smiles, as I know the answer. We drive on in silence.

We arrive at the prisoner exit gate which is different from the visitor's entrance. There is no guard post, just a ten-foot-high steel mesh gate crowned with razor wire glistening in the sun. There's no one in sight. According to the letter, Alf is to be released at 15:00 hours. At exactly three, a small man appears behind the gate holding a suitcase. The mesh steel door rolls sideways enough to enable him to walk through and then closes again and locks with a loud clang.

Alf stands outside the gate. We're the only car in his sight. He doesn't move. I get out of the car, followed by Clarisse. I stand by the car to see what Clarisse will do.

She looks at me and walks slowly toward her father. As she nears him, she stops, and they look at one another for a moment. Then she walks up to him and hugs him to her. My fear of losing Clarisse is finally gone. The two embrace for a long time. I see her whispering to him but can't hear what they're saying. Then they walk slowly toward me and the car. I walk forward and shake Alf's hand, which is damp from wiping away his tears. Clarisse and Alf get into the back seat, and I begin the drive back to Graniteville, looking occasionally into the rearview mirror. We reach the rectory before dusk.

Our New Home

I don't question Clarisse about her relationship with her father, only grateful that they find solace in one another's company. Occasionally, they drive up and picnic together at the rock on Groton Lake.

I've found some peace in my own life as well in my ongoing correspondence with Paolo who keeps promising to visit us in the summers but then claims his thriving bread business keeps him too busy to travel.

With the rectory languishing on the market, the real estate agency suggests I find another place to live so they can make it more "showable." Apparently, Clarisse, Alf, Clem, and I don't "show" well.

Clarisse debuts the idea of buying a rambling, dilapidated, turn-of-the-century camp she's seen listed and remembers from her childhood on Groton Lake. She's delighted to find it lies only a few hundred yards from her rock and is only eighteen miles from my church. According to the real estate offering, it's been unoccupied and on the market for seven years. To our amusement, the hollow acorn shells, pinecones, and dried-up racoon, chipmunk, bat, and mouse turds we encounter put the lie to the agent's "unoccupied" claim.

Clarisse's low offer is accepted the same day. Pooling our sparse resources and my new stipend, we calculate we can meet the modest mortgage payment. But for propriety's sake, we decide it's best if Clarisse takes out the mortgage and is listed as the owner.

A week after the closing on a lovely summer weekend, we all pack up our few things and move to camp. Several days later, I learn in a letter from Boston that I'm to become a circuit-rider, retaining my current parish, and serving two new ones from our new home.

As to Clarisse and I sharing a home, local folk seem content to believe what suits them. For some, she's an illicit but respected partner inspiring the occasional wink, and for others, she's merely a housekeeper or relative. I hear from a colleague who knows of my circumstances — if not my languishing faith — that the new bishop gets more complaints about the African priests the Church is importing to staff empty parishes than about clerical irregularities among his remaining white shepherds. As long as I keep my beliefs to myself, keep my hands off my altar boys, and maintain sacramental theater, it seems I'll be permitted to care for the many people I've come to love in my travels from town to town.

In Graniteville, I offer a Saturday evening Mass at five and a Sunday morning Mass at nine. In Plainfield, I say an eleven o'clock Mass, and in Cabot, a two o'clock Mass followed by confessions and counselling meetings. I hear confessions after Saturday Mass in Graniteville and then return to Plainfield Thursday evening for confessions and counselling. I schedule marriages and baptisms as requested but am always on call for anointing the dying.

Clem and Alf set up their woodshop in a sagging boathouse not far from the house. They suspend their birdhouse fabrication long enough to shore up the interior framing and to relevel the original roofline and replumb the corner posts. They strip the rotting, mossy cedar shingles from the roof, replace a few rotting boards underneath, and reroof the boathouse with tin roofing sheets scrounged from an abandoned barn nearby.

Under Clem's guidance, Alf takes to woodworking with all his mentor's former enthusiasm, slowly assuming more of their thriving business as their income now contributes significantly to our household expenses. But arthritis plagues Clem's joints, and he can no longer piece together and sand his designs that Alf now assembles and finishes. But he enjoys painting and finishing the increasingly imaginative birdhouses. Alf has also begun making custom art frames from exotic hardwoods for a gallery and framing shop in Montpelier and is making a name for himself in the art world.

Clarisse is earning an associate degree in nursing at a local community college and now works as an orderly in palliative care at the Barre hospital. I keep up my prison visits and find myself wishing I could make room in our home for more of the men I've come to know there. The rectory lawn back in Graniteville still sports a large "For Sale" sign with the phone number of a real estate broker in Boston.

Another Family Member

During the remaining months of summer, we fix up and winterize our home. With his new carpentry skills, Alf eagerly joins this effort, making and replacing rotting sills, soffits, and the stair-treads leading up to the veranda. I use my available time to scrape the curling paint from the shiplap siding and just behind me Clarisse applies white paint and dark green to the storm shutters and trim.

After Mass on Sunday in the summer, the four of us sit on a bench Alf fashioned from a nearby fallen ash, enjoying the fresh lemonade Clarisse brews from lemons and diced mint and serves in a white iron-stone pitcher.

That fall, we all attend Clarisse's graduation from nursing school and cheer together when her turn comes to shake hands with the dean as she hands her a diploma. Her new RN status earns her a significant raise at the hospital, and our prospects steadily improve.

One evening at dinner, Clarisse asks for our attention. Clem, who has taken to snoozing upright at the dinner table after finishing his dessert, opens an eye to rejoin us.

"A woman I've been caring for at the hospital died yesterday as I was holding her hand. In her last breath, she asked if I would care for her son. She'd known she was dying for some time but never mentioned him to me before, even though we talked every morning and afternoon when I came in to regulate her IV pain medication.

"After her body was removed from the unit, I asked Claire in social services about her family. According to their admission records, she was a single mom. No one knew who or where her husband was, or if she even had one. Her son, Norman, was seven and, when she entered the hospital for the last time, he went to a foster care agency in Montpelier. I kept hearing her whispered request in my head, and I called the agency and asked if, as a single woman, I might be considered as a foster parent for Norman. They said my unmarried status would not prevent my fostering Norman, but that they would need to review and approve his living circumstances."

Quiet at first, we all understand Clarisse is asking us if we're willing to take another person into our family.

Clem speaks first. "Lord knows, I'll be the next to go. That'll make for some room here, not like we don't have enough. There's that room we'se storin' stuff in next to my room. I could move inta there and give the boy my room as it's insulated nice and warm now and I all'as preferred to sleep cold."

Clarisse suggests we all think on it till the following evening, and we all nod in assent.

The next evening, my confessions run later than usual and I'm again late for supper. I join what's seems a lively conversation. As I help myself to boiled potatoes and a slab of cod, the table goes quiet. On my first mouthful, Alf, says, "Well, we'se waitin' for your vote, Pierre."

"On…? Oh, yes," I answer as I refocus my thoughts from the confessional to the dinner table and the issue at hand. "You've all voted?"

"Ya, but we ain't sayin' 'til you say," adds Alf.

"I think it's a wonderful idea and I'm all for it. You think the foster folks are gonna approve of our idea of family?" I ask Clarisse.

"We'll soon find out," she answers, smiling.

I know now I'm falling in love with this woman.

Clarisse fills out the paperwork and the foster agency schedules a home visit.

The following weekend, we clean and dust all the sawdust from the living spaces. Since I'm known by many in Barre, we agree that any subterfuge about our living conditions would get out, so the day of the visit, I don my cassock and Roman collar.

The woman from the agency identifies herself as Gertrude Bennett. Clarisse, who's taken the afternoon off, invites her in and offers a cup of tea or coffee. Mrs. Bennet declines, preferring, as she says, to get right to work as she has another home visit that day.

"First, I need to know the names and employment status of all who live here with you, and then I need to see the kitchen, the bathroom Norman will use and the room he'll sleep in. "You live here year-round I assume?" she asks Clarisse, "and there are no other children in the house?"

Clarisse answers both questions and then introduces Mrs. Bennett to Alf and Clem who come in on cue from outdoors and then to me. Mrs. Bennett seems surprised to see that I'm a Catholic priest. I explain my parish assignments and then further explain how Clem and Alf came to be here. Clarisse picks up the narrative and explains how she came to be here and that she cares for her father and keeps house for me. Mrs. Bennet seems comfortable with this explanation, but her demeanor, Clarisse and I later agree, is hard to read.

Clarisse shows her around the house, answers a few more questions, signs a form, and then shows her to the door, thanking her for her visit.

The following Friday after her day shift, Clarisse returns home with Norman in tow. He's carrying with both hands a small shellacked valise in front of him that bangs uncomfortably against his knees.

When I return home from Plainfield, the family's already at table. Norman's sitting next to Alf picking at some green beans and a diced hotdog smothered in catsup. I join the table and introduce myself to Norman, who simply nods his head without looking up. Alf introduces him, encouraging him to respond this time.

"Norman, meet Father Pierre. Pierre meet my grandson, Norman."

The following month, Clarisse and I decide to make the five-hour journey to Quebec City with Norman to revisit our heritage and to savor the unknown joys of urban life. We stay in a modest inn along the riverfront in Vieux-Québec that once served as a maritime warehouse. We wander the streets of the old city, dipping into shops, bookstores, and cafes.

On one of our walks we see several posters for a performance of the *Bach Messe en si mineur* in La Basilique-Cathedrale Notre-Dame de Québec. On a whim, we decide to go that evening. Neither of us has any knowledge of the classical repertoire of an earlier Church.

I notice Norman's eyes glancing around the vast and ornate interior of the basilica. I no longer wear my Roman collar and cassock when I'm not serving the Church, so Clarisse feels comfortable taking my hand from my lap and holding it between us on the oak pew. She is holding Norman's hand on her other side. We listen transfixed for almost two hours until the *Agnus Dei* and the final choral notes of the *Dona Nobis Pacem*. After the concert, we're silent, trying to retain the deep sense of peace we feel as we walk with Norman back to our inn.

The next day we sleep in. When we wake, Norman's standing at the window watching the massive lakers transporting Great Lakes iron ore out through the St Lawrence Seaway. We have an early lunch before making the long trip home.

Late in November after the first snow blankets the Groton Lake shoreline, a package arrives with Paolo's return address. Clem is alone in the house and signs for it, painstakingly block lettering his first name and his prisoner number as he had done in prison. The postman looks at it, makes no comment, and leaves. Clem sets the package on the couch and returns to his chair, where he now spends most of his days. His arthritis has crippled his hands and knees, and he can no longer work with Alf in the boathouse. After a week of watching and advising Alf from a steel stool, Clem has moved inside for good and settled into a winged arm chair in the corner. We all sense, but avoid mention of, his obvious decline.

The cold winter further compacts our family. Four days straight of thirty-degrees-below-zero mornings have us all huddling around the Prussian General woodstove that provides all our heat. The work we've done insulating walls, attic, and cellar retains much of the stove's warmth, even as we hear the many small creatures who share our home rustling in the walls and rearranging insulation to create nests and caches for their own winter food stores.

Alf and Norman have moved Clem's metal frame bed into the living room by the stove, so he can stay warm and not climb stairs which tax his limited mobility.

Night-chills overcome his love of "sleeping cold." Clarisse sets him up in his chair for the daylight hours and then helps him into his bed when we all retire.

On the day I leave early to celebrate the Annunciation in my three churches, Clem doesn't wake up. I learn this late in the afternoon when I return. Clarisse has called the local funeral home but asked them not to pick up Clem's body until after I return so I can say my goodbyes and offer last rites to this gentle man who has yet to forgive himself for the murder of the man who caused his logging horse such pain.

I ask for and receive local permission to bury Clem at home. Tuesday, Clem's borne home in a hearse and rests peacefully in an open oak casket Alf's made for him. It rests on two sawhorses on our front porch. We thank the funeral service for their help and the heavily chromed black hearse drives off in a cloud of blue exhaust. We each say our good-byes alone and later together in a service I piece together both from the liturgy and our love and sorrow for Clem's leaving us.

Spring had come early this March and the ground easily gave up its soil before we lower Clem into the moist shoreline soil next to the boathouse he loved.

Transubstantiation

I'm no longer the person I once knew, nor the priest I wanted to be. In fact, I no longer know who I am.

Norman sometimes accompanies me on my rounds when he's not in school. In fourth grade now, he's come alive in the company of other boys his own age. In summer, they organize fishing expeditions around Groton Lake and have made a secret map of all their favorite trout pools. Clarisse makes them cheese and tomato sandwiches and a thermos of her lemonade to take with them. In the shop, Alf has built a lapstrake trapper boat that he and Norman often fish in.

Norman sometimes accompanies me to Mass in spite of Clarisse's mild objections. She's not anxious for him to practice my faith or to become an altar boy as I was but seems comfortable having him attend church occasionally and learn right from wrong in another setting and see people come together to help one another in times of need. I appreciate her trust in me.

I ask her one night before we fall asleep if I'm Father Pierre or Norman's father. She smiles and kisses me goodnight, answering only, "That's for you to decide."

Paolo's packages now come quarterly and contain a bottle of the abbey's signature red wine and several loaves of his einkorn sourdough bread. Clarisse is amused at the idea that my friend, a man of God, is comfortable breaking the law so consistently by shipping wine through the postal system. We're both amused by the arrival of bread and wine in our home and suggest that, beyond sustenance, it's our family communion.

One day while Alf and his "grandson" are out laying flies over their favorite fishing hole with two bamboo fly rods Clarisse bought them, Clarisse suggests we go for a swim. Carrying only her signature lemonade and two plastic cups, we head down the path to her rock. She sets down the cups and thermos and dives in. After donning my trunks, I follow and sidestroke out to where she's treading water.

"Will you marry me?" I ask.

"If you want to," she answers. "You won't be the first married priest, I suspect, but you'll certainly be the first priest I've ever married."

The following weekend with Norman and Alf standing by us on the rock, Alf gives his daughter to me in marriage and Norman hands us the rings we bought for each other at a craft shop in Montpelier. After the simple service in which we promise only to love one another for another day, I bless a loaf of Paolo's bread and a bottle of his wine and we all tear pieces from the loaf and wash it down with some red wine from china teacups.

Norman and Al head off later in the trapper boat to do some fishing and Clarisse and I go home and make love for the first time.

I don't miss my childhood faith but am no less happy for being an agnostic priest. Having shed the bounds and artifice of conjured faith and shame, I'm free to enjoy and love those I meet on their terms and I no longer dread an eternal afterlife.

Ego me absolvo.

AFTERWORD

When I was three, my war-widowed mother remarried into a French-Canadian family, I converted along with her to Catholicism and was baptized into a small parish in northern Vermont. I became an altar boy at eight, knew the Mass in three languages by ten, and was confirmed by the bishop at twelve with a firm slap on the cheek.

At thirteen, I went away to Phillips Exeter Academy. On arriving, I was introduced to my roommate who looked me up and down and asked, "What are you?" I answered, I'm sorry, I don't know what you mean." He explained, "Like what race, what religion?" I answered, "Catholic." He looked disappointed. To be polite, I asked what he was, and he answered, "I'm a Jew." "What's a Jew?" I asked.

Schubart is a German-Jewish name. I was born into the *Our Crowd* contingent of assimilationist Manhattan Jews, anxious to differentiate themselves from the bearded, black-hat shtetl Jews of the Lower East Side.

When I was twelve, I asked my paternal grandmother what her religion was, and she answered, "Ethical Culture." I ticked through the white churches in my Vermont home town and no such church came to mind. I asked where her church was, and she said on WQXR (the city's classical music station) Saturday morning, leaving me even more confused about my family.

In my third year, a classmate and I designed a class with Colin F.N. Irving, who taught Russian History. Our goal was to read all pre-revolutionary Russian literature currently in translation. Among many titles we read in the first year was Dostoevsky's *The Brothers Karam`azov*. When I finished *The Legend of the Grand Inquisitor,* an interior tale told by Ivan, the rationalist-atheist to his brother Alyosha, a novice Orthodox monk, I turned away from the Church and never looked back.

Still, three of my closest male friends have been priests. The first was Père Omer Dufault, my parish priest when I was very young, with whom I maintained a lifelong friendship. The second was Father Jim Dodge, a high Episcopalian, who after graduating from Cornell and becoming a champion single-sculler, announced to his conservative parents he was joining the Catholic Church where he became a Trappist monk to study under Thomas Merton. A decade later he left the Abbey and became the spiritual advisor to the von Trapp Family in Stowe, but after a disagreement with the Baroness over her request to serve glühwein in the chapel, came to live for four years in the basement of our home.

The third was Father Bob, whom I met in an eating disorder treatment facility. I weighed about 480 pounds. Father Bob weighed just under 700 pounds and arrived there on a gurney when I first met him. He lost some weight but died not long after we met. Not one of these dear friends ever tried to convince me to return to the Church.

– Bill Schubart